MEA NICO

a novel

DONNA LEE DAVIS

for all the cheerful givers

"I solemnly assure you, the man who has faith in me
will do the works I do, and greater far than these"

–John 14:12, New American Bible

I

Nicaea[1], August 25, 325 A.D.

No light in the prison cell. No light, only varied depths of darkness. Shallow dimness through daylight hours when surely the sun blazed outside, betrayed by thin rays raining dust motes, the intermittent glimmers of noon-bright that seeped through cracks above his head. Or when the door through which he was fed slid open, revealing a hand and half-light duskiness beyond it. But the nights, the endless nights were deep, fathomless, fraught with guilt and wearing a veil of darkest, smothering blackness. The nights were interminable, for sleep rarely came. Or if it did he was insensible of it, for all was the same, a crushing, endless empty sameness, and no consciousness of rest. Life was reduced to counting breaths, breathing prayer, craving the glow from the stub of just one candle. Ever a longing for remembered light.

No sound in the prison cell, save infrequent cries from others, muffled and muted through thick walls of stone slabs. Others who perhaps had no faith at all for solace, no prayers, no hope to sustain them. Many men, he realized, who were far more lost than he. He tried to remember to pray for them, especially when his own need was keen. His petitions for the others were gifts made in secret, as was his dearest custom.

This was not his first imprisonment. One might say he had long ago perfected confinement skills. For comfort—for sanity—he talked to himself, but never aloud. There would be no biting of words into the stale, foul air,

---

1 ancient Greek city in northwest Anatolia (Asia Minor)

1

words for his ears alone. There was only a voice within himself, speaking from head or heart to soul and back again, the whisper of self-knowledge. A communion of the spirit, as it were. And because there was little satisfaction and nothing new in that exchange, there lingered a hunger for communication, for conversation. Ever a yearning for remembered words.

That was his whole existence now, darkness, pain and silence. Yet this night, this longest, blackest, most unendurable night, he heard—he was sure he heard, from outside himself—a call, his name, the words from his childhood, lovingly expressed. "Nico, Nico." Was it real? Was it to be trusted? Did he truly hear someone? *Nico, Nico! Mea Nico!*

II

Patara,[2] Lycia, 270 A.D.

There was light aplenty at the beginning, light and voices and music. His earliest memories were of a sweet brilliance, a round moon face lit by lantern shine near his crib, and a soft crooning sound that was care and safety personified. How warm it was, if he was chilled; how cool and refreshing if he were hot. How that face and that voice was his world, and how his world was a place of sustenance and contentment. There were other faces, soft like hers or long and bearded; other sounds in the breeze that blew from the Mediterranean Sea, fragrant and steady; other songs, other words. But what he remembered most was her fragrance of musk and cinnamon; her touch, commanding yet gentle; her smile in the lantern light. Her words: *Mea Nico.*

He could not know it then, but the attentions of his moon faced nurse were a source of contention between his mother and father and were of troubling curiosity to his esteemed uncle, a consecrated bishop.

"Is it not unnatural, my sister, that this woman should have such attachment to the babe?" Methodius stroked his long whiskers thoughtfully. They had been standing near the threshold of the nursery chamber, hidden by shadows, watching the woman cradling and cooing to the infant child. His brotherly concern was well meant; he prided himself on his ability to observe and assess situations yet refrain from judgments. "It is as though she casts herself into your role as his mother."

---

2 ancient city on the southwest coast of modern day Türkiye (Turkey)

Johanna stiffened somewhat and drew her palla[3] reflexively over breasts which after more than a month were still sore and weeping. "A wet nurse was a necessity, I assure you, Methodius, and we were fortunate to find Nonna both available and willing. She does not usurp my role, but merely enhances it." She eyed the bronze cross on the heavy chain about her brother's neck and recognized the mild yet unmistakable authority with which he carried himself, even in her familiar presence. "Are you quite sure that it is not that she is Roman born? That is my husband's objection. She is a Christian, of that I am certain, and a woman fluent in both Latin and Greek. Where were we to find a handmaid more suitable?"

"Where indeed." Methodius smiled faintly. "I am not anti-Roman, my dear, but only anti-heresy. Perhaps that is what worries Epiphánios. There are factions, particularly in Rome, which would sully the purity of our Lord's word, should we let them."

"You give my husband undeserved credit. He has not your spiritual gifts nor a ready understanding of theological matters. His prejudices are merely that; he sees the Romans, as a race, as brutish conquerors."

"And he does not wish his household to be conquered?"

"Exactly so," she said, amused. The nurse had lain the child in his crib. "My son sleeps. Come! You must have something to eat. The journey on foot from your dwelling place is draining. You surely are famished."

He brightened. "I confess, from the moment the Patara lighthouse came into view, not to mention the yellow stones of this blessed house beyond, I could think of little but your excellent gastrin."[4]

"You always had a preference for sweets, Methodius. I fear you are but a boy beneath that beard."

"And what is wrong with that?" he smiled. "A man who honors his youth preserves his innocence."

---

3 cloak
4 ancient form of baklava, a Greek pastry

"'And from innocence is born humility,' yes, I remember."

She led him away from the darkened nursery to the bright central courtyard, gliding regally, trailing a colorful costume of rich silk as befit her station. She was a handsome woman even now, weakened as she had been by a difficult birth. Her features were delicate, her face nearly unlined, her silvered hair pinned in becoming swirls that were thick and glossy. And she was an accomplished woman. Orders had been issued upon her brother's arrival, so that the meal was already in place, hearty dishes of salted fish, olives, teganites[5] with honey, and figs. Her dear husband too was ready to break his fast and greeted the bishop with deference and affection.

"Methodius, brother, you look well."

"As do you, Phánios. Fatherhood becomes you."

Epiphánios, solidly built and equal to his wife in comeliness, seemed to swell in stature with the compliment. The men embraced and took their places before the repast, while Johanna withdrew to her seat in the shade at the rim of the courtyard. Like any woman of means in Lycia, she avoided the sun to preserve a pale complexion; and in the old Greek custom, she would eat after the men had their fill.

From her vantage point beneath a prized liquid amber[6] she could listen to their discussion while finishing the embroidery in her lap. Their topic was, as she knew it would be, whether her infant son should be baptized now or after he had attained an age for instruction. Her brother argued for the former with all the strength and persuasion of his position in the Church. Her husband, a simple man of business and logic, favored the latter course. To Johanna's mind, the question was already decided. Had she not borne this miracle child late in life, after her husband's loins had nearly lost all vigor and after she had nearly lost all hope? Would she allow this precious soul she had long prayed for to be left vulnerable to the evils of the world for one day

---

5 pancake made with wheat flour and curdled milk
6 sweetgum tree

longer than need be? Was she not the beating heart of this household, and as its mistress had she not already prepared the site and the means?

Johanna looked up from her stitching, seeing not what was before her but in her wistful mind's eye all that was beyond her courtyard walls. She loved Patara. This was the city where she had been betrothed to Epiphánios as a young girl. She loved the thick groves of cedars of Lebanon, the beach of blue waves, the amethyst fields of bougainvillea and the wild strawberry trees, the lighthouse, the Date Palm Baths. These were home, as much as the ochre stones of these walls were a refuge. These were her son's heritage. How wonderful it would be to see him publicly baptized in the sea itself or in the yellow Xanthos River. But as Christians in a pagan land under Roman rule they must be circumspect. It would not do to make a spectacle, to call attention.

Sighing, she continued embellishing a tiny tunic for her son. The baptismal garment, white on perfect white. A large basin of copper and chiseled quartz had been prepared, with a gravity fount fashioned to provide moving, living water. The water would be not too cold, nor too warm; she had seen to that. All was ready. She needed only that the men in her life reach a decision and believe it was their own.

"I suppose there is value in early baptism," her dear Phánios was saying at last, helping himself to another fig. "It is done increasingly often in our community; it is accepted. I bow to your authority, Methodius."

She smiled.

Thus it came to pass that on the third day of his uncle's visit, in the full sun of their home courtyard and in the sight and hearing of friends who practiced The Way of the Christ, the Holy Spirit came to dwell in his infant soul.

"What name do you give your son?" Methodius asked.

"Nicolaos," said his father.

The bishop passed his little body clad in the purest white through the flow of water three times, in the name of the Father, and of the Son, and of the Holy Spirit.

From her place behind the first circle of friends the servant Nonna, watching intently, nodded approval and silently mouthed the words, "Mea Nico."

III

Birdsong in the morning. He was five years old and maddeningly obsessed with birdsong in the morning. "Is it the blackbird, Mama, or could it be the skylark?" Not waiting for an answer, perhaps sensing that she had none. "Nonna says the skylark only sings like that on the wing, so I think it is the blackbird, for I do not see any bird flying. Every morning the same song, and Nonna says the blackbird is always the first to call the day." His little face dimmed with doubt. "Yet it could be the lark. I will ask Nonna."

"'Nonna!' Really, Nicolaos, your Nonna does not know everything."

"Oh, but she does, Mama."

She shook her head, a firm no. "These are questions for your tutors."

"My tutors are great scribes and can teach from many scrolls, but Nonna knows all the stories of the beauty in God's world."

"Nevertheless." This child. His chatter was incessant, his questions probing, his imagination boundless and often the ruler of his very being. "Do not let your father hear you laud Nonna on the subject of birds or stories or any other thing. He pays those tutors to instruct you."

"But is not Nonna also paid, Mama? You have told me many times that she is not of our family."

"She is paid," Johanna snapped. "She is rewarded with a place in our household. A place of honor, if I may say."

The boy was quiet for a moment. Appeased, perhaps, or more likely forming another round of questions. She felt instant regret for her tartness with him. He was such a dreamy eyed innocent, so full of life and love, and still so very much her miracle babe. He was divinely formed, in her estimation. A sweet face crowned with dark curls that revealed fair lights in the sun. She marveled yet again how she and Phánios, both of them rusting and graying, could have produced such a wonder.

"Do you know the bee-eater, Mama?"

"The merops, yes. They trouble the hives."

"But they are pretty birds, so many colors, and they eat other bees and wasps that are harmful, and yet they are not stung. And sometimes they bathe in water, and sometimes they take dust baths." Slowing for a breath, "I do not think I would like a dust bath."

"No, nor I."

"Nonna says that God made every living thing. She says even those that seem bad have some good in them, and though we think some creatures ugly, there is much beauty in them. We need only to look at them with God's eyes."

Johanna caressed the silken top of his head. He raised it and looked at her. The teeth in his smile were perfect pearls, she thought; his eyes were brown as two chestnuts and full of love.

Across the wide courtyard Nonna of Rome, daughter of Marcus Cornelius, young widow of Theophánes the Greek, regarded the overcast sky with disappointment. She welcomed the soothing warmth of the sun and, unlike Johanna, often chose to perform her duties where its rays could bathe and enliven her. Daily she rubbed olive oil scented with cinnamon into her skin as had her mother before her, deepening the russet hue that her Theo had found to his liking. This was only one of the many things her mistress frowned upon that to Nonna were as natural as breathing. Another was any open demonstration of the bond she felt with the son of the house, Nicolaos.

This was a strange and trying foreign land, this Lycia. Part of the empire, yes, but so unlike her city of Rome. The Lycians had their own history, their own customs and prejudices. And these Greek Christians living among them were different in their worship, which was dry and brittle as old bones. She sorely missed the anthems of her youth and the fellowship she had known. But had not the Apostle Paul, she reminded herself, come here to Patara in a merchant ship just as she had? And were these Greek followers of The Way not as worthy of the graces of the Christ as were observant Romans? It had taken a measure of courage and trust in God to follow her seafaring husband here. It took even more to survive Theo's death in his prime while their child was still in her belly; even greater faith to face the loss of that child in still-birth. When the care of Nicolaos was offered to her, it was a blessing from a merciful God. Perhaps her mistress did not see that. Or perhaps she did, and that was the problem.

"Nonna!" the boy called, bounding to her. "I must know, was it truly the blackbird welcoming the day this morning?"

"None other," she smiled. "His song is sweet, is it not?"

"Very sweet. And long! Not just a chirping from tree to tree, but a true song!"

She saw Johanna, dressed in queenly purple, observing from her seat in the shade. She allowed herself a touch, just one touch; one small adjustment to his tunic, before Nico bounded away again.

Birds. In his third summer it had been the sea. He had brought her shells to admire, to explain. They were displayed in her bed chamber even now, whelks and cowries, mussels and bits of clam shells and a broken starfish, arranged like artworks, mementos of the best moments of her life. How she loved her boy!

The mistress gathered the folds of her regal chiton,[7] rose gracefully and went inside the house, taking Nicolaos with her. In the thick of a small tamarisk beside her, Nonna noticed a spider toiling tirelessly, weaving a trap or a home. Perhaps Nico's next fascination would be with such creatures; the world was alive with so much for a boy to learn. For several minutes she watched the little spider work, spinning a web of enticement. Clouds moved at last and sunlight caught the filament, burnishing it. For one glorious moment not a web or a danger but a delight. For one glorious moment, pure gold.

---

7 full-length garment

IV

The Bishop of Patara frequented his sister's home freely and more often after her son's baptism, and more often still as the child approached the age of reason. There was something about Nicolaos that drew the uncle, fascinated him. The boy was the first of their blood, as well as in the line of Epiphánios, to be born in decades; the last of their blood who would carry all their fortunes into the future. From the time Nicolaos could walk and talk he was special, any fool could see that. The birth of this child inspired reflection upon how the Lord Jesus Christ had come into the world as a helpless babe. And as Nicolaos grew, he appeared to exhibit a natural piety. He, Methodius, consecrated bishop of Christ, would see that this innocent lamb was properly reared in The Way.

To that end at every opportunity he pressed his brother-in-law on his intentions for the child.

"There must be education, Phánios."

"Of course."

"Not merely a litterator[8] and later a grammaticus,[9] but proper instruction in philosophy."

"And so a rhetor[10] as well, I suppose," countered Epiphánios, his eyebrows raising with mirth.

"Do you doubt that your son will be capable of higher education?"

---

8 teacher of reading, writing, basic math
9 tutor in writing and speaking skills, poetry analysis
10 tutor in oratory, geography, geometry, literature, music, philosophy

"No, no, of course not," Epiphánios said, sobering. "He is an intelligent child."

Methodius nodded. "Intelligent, yes. But gifted, I think."

"Ah?"

"When he is ready, I myself will undertake his training in philosophy."

"Ah."

"And if he is so inclined, in theology."

And there it was. Not a career in business, then; Nicolaos was not to follow his father's path. Epiphánios noticed his wife, sitting quietly in her corner, looking supremely content. She was the jewel of his existence, but must she and her family outshine him at every turn? He sighed. There were small battles in life that merited a struggle. This was not one of them.

"If he is so inclined, brother," he said, somewhat wearily. "And as usual, I accede to your wisdom. Shall we drink to it?"

Proof that she had been listening closely, Johanna summoned a servant and called for wine. It was the very best their region had to offer. Not the watery drink appropriate to a philosopher's or a priest's table but the very best Epiphánios, successful man of business, could buy.

V

When Nicolaos was six years old, nearly seven, Nonna was sent away. He was told by his father and mother that she had returned to Rome to remarry. He listened to them patiently and was respectful of them, but he did not believe what they said. He looked for her everywhere and fretted that Nonna had somehow been stolen or suffered some bad end; else how could she have gone without bidding him farewell? But when he saw that she had not left behind her seashells, even the broken starfish, he knew that she had left willingly, and taken the tokens of his heart with her. Somehow that was consoling.

He began to spend more time at prayer, speaking to God as his dearest friend, just as Nonna had taught him. It made him feel less lonely. And when he was seven, nearly eight, God sent him Clodio.

Clodio was a lad like him, perhaps a year or two older, a Lycian whose forebears had turned from the worship of Apollo around the time the Apostle Paul had come through Anatolia.[11] There was much about him that that was Lycian, and much that was Roman. He knew the world—their city of Patara—very well and liked to share his knowledge of it, particularly when they could explore together. And everywhere he looked, Clodio recognized the hand of God; in that, he was much like Nonna.

Their friendship was hesitant at first. Nicolaos was the only son of a wealthy house, a pupil of scribes, and the nephew of a bishop. Clodio had an amazing number of siblings, came from a long line of fishermen and bakers, and drew his knowledge from the streets. He was olive skinned and black

---

11 Asia Minor

haired, sturdy and angular, taller than Nicolaos by far. Quick witted and cool headed, he was always ready for sport and discoveries. Their association was a revelation to them both. Merely boys at play to begin, when both were young children—hoops and balls, racing and wrestling—but as they grew older and closer, youths whose ripening friendship was fraught with lessons which could not have come from schooling.

The home of Clodio was humble and plain, teeming with children, full of laughter. The sights and smells were different from those Nicolaos was accustomed to, the food more coarse, the discipline lax. The bread made by Clodio's mother was that which was fed to the staff of the house of Epiphánios and to the slaves in other households, but after a morning's play in the sea air, it was deliciously nourishing.

And just as new surroundings expanded his own perspective, Nicolaos delighted in broadening the experiences of his friends. With Johanna's blessing he would bring baskets of unexpected treasures to Clodio's mother after assembly on the odd Lord's Day, enough for the family. Imported fruits and sweetmeats, white bread made from finely milled wheat flour; sometimes a dish of spiced boar or roasted stag—foods commonplace at home, rendered somehow exotic when shared. He would return home with fresh fish or herbed goat cheese for his mother's kitchen, and words of thanks and blessing committed to memory.

Through scrolls borrowed from his lessons, Nicolaos helped Clodio improve his reading. And as self-appointed guide in their roaming the city and through his gift for stories, Clodio educated Nicolaos about Lycia.

"I was born under the sign of the scorpion," Clodio proclaimed jovially, while they climbed the rocky embankment near the city gates.

"The sign?"

"Do your teachers not tell you of the zodiac?"

"I have heard of it," Nicolaos said. "My tutors are teaching me Scriptures. I think the wise men who visited the child Jesus studied the stars."

"Your natal day is under Pisces the fish, Nicolaos. You are at home with the sea and all waters, while I roam the land."

"It is true, I love the sea and the beach. But your father is a fisherman!"

"And I am not my father!" grinned Clodio. "The scorpion is also a water sign. But I prefer woods and hills, and the stones of the city beneath my feet."

"The scorpion. Have you a stinger, then?"

"Oh, aye!" They scrimmaged in fun for a moment, Clodio swinging about, thrusting an imaginary sword-like appendage, Nicolaos nimbly evading the strikes.

They had reached the arched gates and the head of Apollo toppled in an earthquake in the time of Emperor Antonius Pius,[12] its beauty intact but its expression quizzical by virtue of its lopsided attitude. Taking seats on a sandstone pedestal bench, the boys went unnoticed by men hurrying past. It was a fine bright day with high clouds. A man leading a horse passed from the main gate. Another herding a flock of sheep entered, as did bearers with their burden, a canopied litter draped in gaudy striped cloth and mystery.

They were surrounded by the grandeur of the city, so old in its stones and carvings, its tombs etched into the cliffs. Clodio had explained that the ancients believed their souls would be transported to the afterlife by a winged creature, and so placed their tombs on the cliff edges all along the Lycian coast, the better to have their spirits flown away. Yet Patara was also new and full of life in its markets, amphitheaters and baths, colorful life that excited a boy's fantasy. Below them stretched the beach and blue sea. Rising above them, brown dunes and green hills, and distant mountains.

"It is wonderful," Nicolaos said. "I think I shall never know all of it."

"All of what, Nicolaos?"

"The world, and all it has to offer. If you are a scorpion, I am the sea turtle, carrying my house on my back."

---

12 141 A.D.

Solemnly, Clodio considered a moment. "Certain, yours is a great and heavy house. But I think you will yet go far and see amazing things, if God wills it."

Nicolaos smiled at that. God had sent him a friend indeed.

VI

"Today we shall visit my bride," Clodio announced on another fine cloudless day when Nicolaos was twelve.

"Have you a bride?" asked Nicolaos, incredulous.

His friend flashed a bright smile. "I do indeed. We were betrothed five years ago," he said. "Our mothers wished it, and our fathers arranged it." Lycian women were much more forward than Greek women, Nicolaos had observed. Many Lycian family customs were altogether different. They used their mother's names rather than their father's, for instance; when asked about his lineage, a Lycian gave the name of his mother and the women before her. "Have you been promised, Nicolaos?"

The question bewildered him. "I do not think so."

Clodio regarded him strangely. "You would know if you were. There is a ceremony and gifts are exchanged."

"This is in church?"

"No, amongst the families. At least, that is the way it is done in ours." They were walking through an unfamiliar part of the city, a darkened stretch of tall crumbling walls closing on a narrow street of rough cobbles. Clodio pulled him out of the way of a lumbering cart and donkey that filled nearly the width of the road. "I do not remember much about my ceremony, but I remember that I liked her," he said. "I am lucky. My father was betrothed at the age of five and never met my mother until their marriage day." He pulled a wry face and laughed. "Or perhaps he also was lucky, in truth, for they have certainly made up for it since."

Nicolaos knew vaguely that he was speaking of the number of children the union had produced, and felt himself coloring slightly. "What is her name, your bride?"

"Vivienne. Is it not a pleasant sound?"

He nodded.

"When she is of age and I am a man and have prepared a home, her father will pay a dowry, our betrothal will be announced before the assembly in the church, and we will be married." He looked extremely pleased with himself. "You will be there," he added confidently.

"I will?"

"Of course. You will witness the vows." He yanked at his friend's tunic again, this time to pull him away from a pile of rags in a doorway. A dirty hand reached up from the pile, which Nicolaos realized was not merely rags but a beggar. "We have no money," Clodio declared loudly as they passed.

Nicolaos looked back over his shoulder at the shuddering pile and the receding hand. "He is hungry?" he asked.

"Naturally he is hungry. If a man cannot work or will not work, he will go hungry. Patara has many like him. The poor will always be among us. It says so in the Scriptures, does it not?"

Nicolaos, who had been tutored in the Scriptures since he was five, could have countered that Jesus also told his disciples to feed the poor, but he held his tongue.

They walked on, until the narrow walled road opened onto a broad street lined with cypresses, and they soon arrived at a modest dwelling smaller and somewhat finer than Clodio's. They were welcomed by Vivienne and her mother, invited into their tiny courtyard, and treated to honey cakes and goat's milk in the fragrant shade of a jasmine covered portico. The girl was pretty to look at and shy, with light eyes and long light brown hair in a braid. She showed them a sage green and crimson rug she was working with the motif of hares and arrows, and they played a lively game of knucklebones together.

It was an agreeable way to pass an afternoon. Vivienne lost some of her shyness as they played, and she had a bubbling laugh, which was what he would remember best about her. But at home again and all that night, Nicolaos was burdened with thoughts of the beggar's outstretched hand, rough with callouses and gray with dirt. And with the thought of hunger. True hunger, which he was sure he himself had never felt.

Alone in their bed chamber a night and day later, Johanna gnawed surreptitiously at her nails and the skin around them, something she tended to do when nervous. It was an atrocious habit, one which she hoped to overcome eventually, should she live long enough. She must apprise her husband of certain facts concerning their son, and she was apprehensive in the extreme. She heard Epiphánios approaching on the stairs; his tread was heavy, his breathing labored. Steeling herself, she self-consciously sat on her hands. It would not do to appear apprehensive before him. It simply would not do.

He entered and without a glance at her began to disrobe. She should avert her eyes, but what was modesty between those long married?

"Phánios," she began, "I must tell you what our Nicolaos has asked today."

"Ah?"

"Phánios, he asked if he was betrothed."

He turned around. "Eh?"

"Or if he was to be betrothed." She was perspiring; she could not conceal her concern.

"And what did you tell him?"

"I? I did not say."

He looked full at her then, took in the worry, the anguish in her eyes, and burst into hearty laughter. "Did you not quote your brother, 'If we are to come to the likeness of God, we must aspire to the virginity of Christ'?"[13]

"Oh, Phánios, no!"

He saw that she was near tears and, ceasing his laughter, sat down beside her. "What, then? Was he uneasy about it, intent upon it, or only curious?"

"Curious, I think."

He put his arm about her and gently pulled her close. "Tomorrow I will tell him how we were promised to each other, and how to us it was a blessing. But I will also say that there are other blessings, other ways to live, and that each must find his own path."

She relaxed at last, her head nestled on his shoulder.

"There is more," she confided.

"More?"

"He saw a beggar, and was moved to promise God that he will fast on Wednesdays and Fridays. And he will take food on other days only after you and I have made our daily devotions."

Epiphánios held her away from him that he might search her earnest eyes, feeling the weight of his own girth a reproach. He had to laugh again, in spite of himself. Was there no end to the boon of fatherhood?

---

13 Hero-Martyr Methodius, Bishop of Patara, a saint in Orthodoxy, taught that Jesus Christ remained a virgin His whole life as an example for men.

VII

The continued natural piety of his nephew had not gone unnoticed by Bishop Methodius. He received frequent detailed and favorable reports from the boy's tutors, as well as breathless accounts from his sister, who seemed bewildered and somewhat in awe of her own child.

"I cannot comprehend it, Brother. Phánios and I provide a devout example and are not stinting in our charity, but Nicolaos! Nicolaos would have us ever do more, pray more, give more. Am I to be shamed in my own house?"

"Sister, I cannot tell whether you are truly vexed or overcome with awe."

"Perhaps both. We are all called to be saints, he says."

"It is so."

"I do not understand where the intensity of his faith comes from. It is humbling and yet frightening."

Methodius placed his hand on Johanna's forehead. "Do not be troubled, woman. Be frightened for him, yes, for the Lord's way is not easy. But be thankful." He regarded her with compassion. "You know that I recognize the light of Christ in your son. I am prepared to guide him. Are you anxious that he come to me?"

"Oh, no!" she exclaimed. Nicolaos to leave his home, her bosom? The very thought could not be borne. "No. When he is ready, and should he feel called, but only then."

He nodded his understanding. "A strong faith and stringent discipline are to be celebrated, so long as the boy is not obsessed with duty and finds joy in life." He gazed at Johanna patiently. He had reports of all his nephew's activities. "He has joy?"

She thought of her son's beaming brown eyes and the delight in them when she presented him with small gifts to take to his friends. "He has joy, Methodius."

The bishop gave his sister his blessing and sent her home.

It was his strong conviction that his young nephew potentially could become a disciple for the ages and a credit to the Church; he felt that the signs were clear. Godliness in one so young was rare and therefor worthy of respect. Neither was he unhappy with the alliances the boy had developed in the city, for such friendships ripened empathy, which was the foundation for service.

Returning to the work he had set aside upon his sister's arrival, he took up pen and ink and began to write, "A time will come when the enemies of Christ will boast, 'We have subjected the earth and all its inhabitants, and the Christians cannot escape our hands.'"[14] Pausing again, he bowed his head to pray that Nicolaos and his generation of believers would survive the test that was sure to come.

His sister was still perplexed. Beneath the parasol clutched by the maid-servant maintaining appropriate distance, Johanna on her way home reflected how her life had changed since becoming a mother. She and Phánios had adjusted quickly enough to the regimen their son had requested of them. They had neglected morning and evening prayer in the past, and she could not deny that joining in regular, thoughtful devotions had brought them closer. Nicolaos was her joy, but Phánios was her love, her life. She drew on

---

14 from the prophetic writings of Hero-Martyr Methodius

his strength, was still stirred by his manliness, and basked in his quiet admiration. But she had to admit to loneliness at times.

Influenced by her son, she had begun visiting the poorer families among the Christian assembly, trying to meet their simple needs, feeding those most hungry, even nursing their sick. But although the Church taught that all were equal in the sight of God, she found she could not regard them so, or allow herself the degree of familiarity that Nicolaos encouraged with his acquaintances. She was kind but aloof; she felt her station in life demanded that.

Business frequently took Phánios away, Nicolaos kept busy with his studies, and there was often no one with whom to share intimacy. She could speak freely to her brother despite his holy calling, but she could not make him understand her, any more than could her husband. What did any man know of a mother's love or a woman's fears at this time of life?

She had no women friends, only female servants, and very few of those. A cook; a laundress and kitchen helper; this gangly girl beside her to keep their rooms clean, to dress her hair and accompany her when she ventured into the city, as propriety required. The size of her household staff was hardly extravagant, given her husband's wealth; and the staff was fairly compensated for their work. But these people were not her equal in birth, education or womanly graces. They were not confidantes.

She sighed heavily. Surely this was right; surely this was the life intended for her. Of those to whom much is given, much is expected. That, she was sure, was established in Scripture. And in giving her Phánios and Nicolaos, God had made her very rich indeed.

Albeit a tad lonely.

VIII

Nicolaos knew nothing of his uncle's plans for him. He knew only that he loved his Lord Jesus Christ, who was his companion in all things. Daily he praised the Lord Jesus, gave thanks for abundant blessings, and asked for direction and wisdom. Oftentimes the direction he sensed in response to prayer took him to Clodio and their ambling escapades. Nearly as often it brought him to the sea. On the happiest of occasions the two destinations were entwined, and the boys passed their free time near the shore.

Clodio preferred to avoid the beach below the lighthouse where he might find the fishing boats used by his father, brothers, uncles and cousins and could be pressed into work he found distasteful. But Nicolaos loved to visit the vessels owned by his father, which were moored near the granaries and gates of commerce. The sailors knew him as "the young master" and made him welcome among them. They taught him the principles of navigation and showed him the intricate utility of knots and the importance of mending sails. Their posca[15] was freely shared, and their gambling games with dice were open to him. He was treated not as a child but as a youth and future able seaman, and their acceptance was important to him.

One of his father's ships was a corbita, a massive sailing vessel with a central mast and gigantic headsail, and two were smaller merchant galleys equipped with ten oars. The corbita was often away at Antioch or Caesaria or even Carthage or Rome; but when it was in Patara, Nicolaos loved to board it and help with the cleaning of the cargo bays below decks.

---

15 watered wine

"You have an odd notion of entertainment, Nicolaos," Clodio observed. He was assisting—with reluctance—in the sweeping of a portion of the galley where grain had been stored.

"Ah, but Clodio, is it not rewarding to be useful, and in such a place of adventure?"

"Adventure!"

"Aye! Think of the fantastic places beyond our shores, the foreign ports, the strange cargos!" He rested his broom against the hull, caressed the smooth planking above his head, and breathed in the close air. "Smell the salt of the sea, the fragrant spices!"

"I smell tar, barley dust and sour wine," grumbled his friend.

"But at least it isn't fish?"

Clodio grinned. "You are right, Sea Turtle. At least I don't smell fish."

They finished their task and whiled away the rest of the sleepy afternoon seated companionably on the stone wall above the breakwater rubble and the loading dock where the corbita was moored. It was quiet, peaceful. Most of the crew had dispersed to the city. The only sounds were the clinking and creaking of the ship's mooring chains, the rhythmic wash of surf against pilings, and the intermittent cries of birds overhead. Noisy gulls were circling, vying for prey with a flock of marsh harriers from the mouth of the Xanthos. Above them a lone ibis soared silently, its glossy plumage reflecting the sun.

Clodio had picked up a piece of driftwood and was turning it in his hands. "My father knows I do not want to be a fisherman," he said suddenly. "I want to please him, but he knows."

"What would you be?"

"A worker of wood, I think, like the Lord Jesus; or a stone cutter." He held up the driftwood. "Do you see a face in it?"

Nicolaos looked hard. "A cunning cat? A caracal?"[16]

---

16 the Persian Lynx, a small wildcat

Clodio nodded. "A few cuts with my knife to bring forth the likeness, a good rubbing with beeswax, and I will give it to Vivienne."

"A fine gift. She will like it."

"And you, Nicolaos, will you have a sailor's exploits, or be a merchant like your father?"

"Neither, I think."

"What, then?"

"Perhaps a teacher, like the Lord."

"And your father will be pleased?"

"Yes. And my uncle, and my mother."

For a moment the boys sat lost in the same thought, righteousness vying with pride, feeling God's sunlight hot and approving on their shoulders. It was Clodio who gave voice to that thought, with a rakish smile: "Then best of all, the both of us will please our Father in heaven!"

IX

In his sixteenth year two things happened that would alter his life, and both were beyond his control. One was that Diocletian, the soldier turned Roman emperor who had reigned over the East in relative peace for two years with Maximian governing the West, formed a new government, henceforth to be known as the Tetrarchy. The provinces were to be ruled by four emperors and overseen by Diocletian, now to be called Imperator. Lycia would be governed from Nicodemia[17] by Diocletian himself and his subordinate, the Emperor Galarius, who was known to hate Christians and all those who did not worship the gods of Rome. Already the army was being purged of the followers of Christ, Manicheans[18] were subject to new persecutions, and the large Jewish community in Limyra[19] had begun to be fearful.

The other remarkable circumstance was that Nicolaos began to feel the first stirrings of his manhood and all its attendant delight and distress. He was not neglectful of his prayer life, for nearly constant prayer was sustenance to him; but he was surely distracted.

"Will she be there, do you think?" He put this to Clodio. They were on their way to athletic games at the amphitheater near the harbor.

"She?"

"Your sister."

---

17 ancient Greek city far north of Patara; modern day Ismit, Türkiye (Turkey)
18 followers of Manichaeism, a dualistic religious system with Christian, Gnostic and pagan elements
19 a small city but large trade center on the Limyrus River

"Which sister?"

Clodio could be exceedingly dim at times.

"Anika, of course."

"Anika? Little Anika?"

"She is my age."

"No, she doesn't care for the games. And why 'of course'?"

Nicolaos felt himself redden. Could Clodio truly be so blind? The girl was luminous. She was filled with loving kindness. Just to watch her caring for her younger siblings was to witness virtue. And to receive a cheery smile from her was benediction. "I—I think she likes me."

His friend rolled his eyes. "Naturally she likes you. We all like you."

Nicolaos reddened the more.

"You mean"—at last noticing his friend's discomfiture—"you mean you like her?"

"I do, yes!"

They were walking past the bouleuterion[20] of the Lycian League, the beautiful white marble building where for generations the people of this land had attempted to govern themselves. Its façade seemed to wear a patina of dignified futility.

Clodio placed a consoling hand on his friend's arm. "She is promised, Nicolaos."

"Promised?"

"In marriage," he said, not unkindly. "She was betrothed to another the summer she was thirteen."

"But—but that is too young!"

"It is the Lycian way."

---

20 council house

It was the Greek way as well, he had learned. But not the way for him, apparently, in his parents' household; and until very recently it had not mattered to him.

"There are other girls in the Christian assembly who may not be promised," Clodio offered. "Most likely because they have no dowry."

Nicolaos was not interested in other girls, could not be interested in just any girl. Sweet Anika had captured all his attention of late, if not his heart as well. "Yes," he said in listless response, so as to close the subject to further discussion. "There are others."

The games were a blur. Even the antics of the funambulus[21] failed to stir him. His evening meal was tasteless, and his night prayer difficult. Lying in bed, he listened to the rain for what seemed like hours, a steady heavy winter rain, although winter had not yet come. What was it the Prophet Isaiah said? God's ways are not our ways, and His thoughts are not our thoughts. When God's Word pours down like rain, we rest in the promise of our glorious future.[22] Well and good for the ancient prophet, in all his wisdom. But what future was there for him? What was his promise?

The moon was high; pulling the rain clouds in its wake, it was moving steadily westward. The hour was late. Turning fitfully yet again and willing himself to clear his thoughts that sleep might come, he resolved to tell his uncle in the morning that he was ready to study theology in earnest.

---

21 tightrope walker
22 Isaiah 55:8-13 NAB, paraphrased

X

Nicolaos did not leave his parents' house but began taking studies three days a week at the bishop's residence. He was amazed at how easily he adapted to this new routine and how comfortable he was with the subject matter and all that was asked of him. His uncle was very kind and extremely patient, and the surroundings were soothing to a lad unused to being away from home.

This imposing building of stone and timbers was situated on the far side of the city, out of sight of the beaches. The lower level was octagonal, the better to signify the eight beatitudes and the resurrection of Christ on the eighth day, and it was open and commodious. That spaciousness was needed, because it was used for Christian assembly on the Lord's Day. The Bishop of Patara was a prolific author and eloquent speaker who drew crowds from regions well beyond these environs. But the upper rooms, the bishop's domicile, were smaller, informal, warm and inviting, littered with a seemingly unending supply of books, scrolls and framed parchments. And here, to his delight, Nicolaos found that the overriding theme of décor was the theology of the sea—the symbols of the fish and the anchor.

"You understand their significance, Nicolaos?"

"Yes, Uncle. Jesus is the anchor of my soul, holding it safe and secure; the cross lies within the anchor."

"And their history?"

"Covert signs of our brotherhood," he answered, without hesitation.

"Never forget," Methodius said, resting a hand on the boy's shoulder. "Never forget that we must be circumspect—you understand this word?"

"Yes, Uncle."

"We must be circumspect even now, within our own community. We may cast our nets for souls but must be mindful of the shoals." He chuckled a bit and stroked his gray beard, pleased with himself. "Souls, shoals, I must write that down."

"Aye, Uncle, it is a wise saying."

The bishop put pen to parchment for a few moments, chuckling again; but when he raised his gaze to his nephew he was wholly serious.

"The holy Ignatius of Antioch, whom I admire, said in his writings, 'Christianity is greatest when it is hated by the world.' But my boy, we must survive to be truly great. We must live in this world and survive it."

About the same time Nicolaos began his studies with his uncle, Clodio sold his first wooden carvings to a merchant with a popular stall in the marketplace. In addition to small animals fashioned from driftwood that were favorites with children, he had built a sturdy sella[23] with rosettes and fanciful figures carved into the legs. All commanded a good price.

"I am on my way," he bragged to Nicolaos. "I will become a fine craftsman, an artisan. Part of the money I will give to my mother, but part I will hide away for myself and Vivienne! We shall have a snug home that will keep out the wind and rain, and a courtyard with many flowers!"

"I am sure you shall. And fill it with many children?"

---

23 stool

"Undoubtedly! Each as comely as their mother and as creative as their father!"

"And I shall instruct them in The Way!"

"Aye," Clodio agreed. "The girls as well as the boys, for all my children will be clever."

They sat in silence for a few minutes in one of their favorite spots near the public wharf, watching the sun beginning to set over the Mediterranean, letting the evening breeze catch their hair and garments. Their times together were less frequent now that each had manly pursuits, but they were no less companionable than in the carefree days of rolling hoops and imaginary swords. A white stork with an impressive wingspan dropped from the orange sky, taking its prey, a water vole; a tiny shriek reached them on the wind. Another silence, more somber than before.

Two Roman soldiers, walking toward them from the direction of the lighthouse that was just now coming alive with evening fire, passed by without so much as a sideways glance.

Clodio waited until they were out of earshot and spoke softly. "Do you really think it will be so for us?"

Nicolaos nodded. "We must only trust." He found a stone shard near his foot and, bending to the sand, drew an arc. He handed the shard to Clodio, who smiled, then drew the corresponding reverse arc, completing the sign of the fish: ICHTHUS in Greek, the letters of which meant the acrostic,[24] "Jesus Christ, God's Son, Savior."

Night was coming on. Sighing and taking leave of his friend, Nicolaos rubbed out the etching with the toe of his sandal. The drawing of a fish was not suspicious in itself, because it was a common symbol among several pagan religions. But he was thinking of his uncle's admonition. The word of the day was "circumspect."

---

24 Iesous (Jesus) CHristos (anointed) THeou (God's) Uios (Son) Sōtēr (Savior)

Their times together were less frequent now that each had
manly pursuits

XI

With the passage of time the hopes and dreams of two youths on the waterfront came near to fruition, even as the wisdom of concealing their plans grew apace. While no one in Lycia anticipated a return to the persecutions Christians had endured in the past, it was well known throughout society that Imperator Diocletian styled himself a "restorer," like Augustus and Trajan before him. His fervent desire was for a return to the "Golden Age of Rome," and he was willing to reform every aspect of public life to achieve his goals. If the elimination of religious minorities was necessary in the pursuit of traditionalism, so be it. It was an unsettling time to be alive if one were out of step with the majority and the prevailing culture. There lurked the latent fear that one's fortune, one's very life, could be cast into jeopardy with little warning.

Clodio had pursued his woodcraft and grown ever more skilled at it. His labors produced wares that were sought after in Patara, Limyra and Myra. With maturity he became a true artisan, engrossed in religious symbolism and devoted to producing works of beauty for Christian assemblies. These too were well received. By the time he was ready to marry he was a man of means. Ruddy and muscular, still nearly a head taller than his friend Nicolaos, his ready smile was his most attractive feature. Clodio was rightly proud of the purse he had accumulated for his household. Every coin was the product of hard work and ingenious trade, and every necessary coin was accounted for.

"I shall make a sacrifice to our assembly as well as the gift of a fine new tabernacle table, and seek their blessing on our union. And Nicolaos, be assured, with Vivienne's dowry added, we shall have more than enough for a good beginning. The holy blessing, good wine and music for dancing, all we have wanted!"

"Indeed, you have done well."

Nicolaos also had succeeded in following his chosen path. He had thrived under his uncle's instruction and earned ever increasing responsibility, first as a reader of Scriptures in the church and later as a deacon.[25] He was as a young man all he had been as a boy, kind and inquisitive, handsome and humble, with an innocent heart attuned to his Lord and eager to be of service. The day that Bishop Methodius anointed him a presbyter[26] by pouring sweet smelling chrism over his head was the happiest day of his life. While fitting the ceremonial stole around his neck his uncle had smiled faintly and said, "You will carry the weight of the people on your shoulders." In the company of their home assembly his father Epiphánios gave voice to the pride he had in his son. Even his mother, through tears of joy and wistfulness, accepted his permanent remove to the bishop's residence.

"You are consecrated now," Methodius had told him, "to be mediator between God and man, to participate in the high priesthood of Jesus Christ. Love God's people as He loves them; preach and teach courageously, and never doubt that He is with you."

---

25 server; assistant
26 elder; priest

And so it came to pass. Just as Clodio had predicted, his good friend witnessed the vows before God which bound him forever to his bride. Indeed, the blessing itself was given at the hand of Nicolaos, holy presbyter, in their accustomed church assembly in lower Patara, within the comforting sight and sound of the sea.

Vivienne had lost her shyness and grown lovelier with each passing year; her laughter was as musical as Nicolaos remembered. Clodio's younger sister Anika, radiant with contentment, was there with her husband and young child. With Clodio's many brothers zealously demonstrating their drinking prowess and their genius for dance, the wedding feast lasted well into the night, under flaming torches thrust into the sands. Johanna and Epiphánios graciously attended, bearing gifts, as did many of the merchants from Patara to whom Clodio was well known. The food was wonderful, roast lamb and pickled fish, olives and cheeses, pasteli[27] and sweetmeats of every description. Musician friends of the young couple plied kithara[28] and trigonon[29] in fault-less harmony; and many a wine-bolstered would-be warbler lifted song to the starry sky. It was a party, as Clodio loudly proclaimed, for the ages.

The joy shared by the new husband and wife was palpable. Nicolaos maintained all evening a happy, inaudible dialog with his Lord Jesus, asking graces and favors for them from on high. And unbeknownst to the new presbyter, God had placed among the guests some acquaintances of the bride who would one day play a significant part in heaven's mysterious plan for Nicolaos, a design that would resonate—as Clodio would have declared, had he known, "for the ages!"

---

27 honey sesame candy
28 7- or 12-stringed lyre
29 Middle Eastern lap harp

XII

The weight of the people. Nicolaos had not often thought about that aspect of his calling until his uncle spoke those words, but it was true. The sea turtle who had carried the weight of his house—his forebears and all their expectations—now carried the weight of his fellow man. He was responsible to them and for them. It was his mission to baptize, to heal and reconcile, to anoint the sick and dying, to teach the Gospel and pour out God's love upon them. He was to be their servant. It brought him to his knees daily.

He happily blessed many couples other than Clodio and Vivienne, and he had seen the assembly's apparent growth in response to his preaching, which was gratifying. What was troubling of late, however, was the increased need for anointing the sick, and the impression that burials were far outnumbering baptisms.

Epiphánios closed his eyes and relaxed in the heated waters rendered azure blue by the painted pattern in reflective tiles. A private bath in his own home was easily his favorite luxury of the several his wealth had afforded him. His wife often preferred the gossip of the women's hour at the nearby public thermae, the Date Palm Baths; and convention prevented their bathing together at home. But Nicolaos often had donned his bathing sandals and tunic and soaked here with his father. Many a lively discussion had taken place in these healing blue waters, and many a restorative hour had been shared in companionable silence. He missed that.

His son had been ensconced at the bishop's residence for a few years now, doing God's work and growing in stature within the Church. Visits home were infrequent and were often ended abruptly when some duty to the assembly or to the bishop called him away. Nicolaos now was a man of consequence, a leader of men, wise beyond his years. Epiphánios had to acknowledge that. Yet to his father's eye, that man was a boy still, a beardless youngster; the same child who had delighted in running barefoot in the surf, the very youth who had once looked to him for guidance.

Meanwhile he himself had grown old. His stubborn joints protested daily. His sight was dimming, his hearing fading. He slept longer hours yet rested less soundly. Having given over much of the responsibility of his business to his steward, he rarely traveled now. These were years which might pass peaceably with his books and his woman, were not that woman intent upon mimicking her son in selfless service to the Church. Rather than concentrating on attending and pleasing her husband, Johanna's leisure time was taken up with visiting the poor and neglected, making Epiphánios feel rather neglected himself.

He heard the rustle of garments, the tap of sandals on marble, and opened his eyes. The paragon of generosity herself was before him, quite unexpectedly. Time had touched Johanna as well, but its mantle sat on her like a royal diadem; her face was lined and her middle thicker, but she was still handsome. It was unlike his wife to drop her veil of false modesty and present herself in the bathing room while he was thus occupied. She was white as marble herself this morning, and trembling.

"What is it? What has you so wrought?"

Johanna sat on the edge of the pool, wringing her hands, holding back tears. "Phánios, the family I served today, there is sickness . . ." She looked away, biting her lip.

"That is why you went to them, is it not?"

She met his eyes, fear and anguish in her own. "I fear it is plague."

Plague! Surely not. Surely—without hesitation he rose from the bath and pulled his wife into his arms.

"You mustn't!" she exclaimed, even as she melted into his wet embrace.

They held each other for several minutes, neither of them speaking. At last she murmured, her voice muffled against his chest, "We must not tell Nicolaos. We must shield him from this."

He closed his eyes again. How quickly life can be turned upside down. "Agreed."

XIII

Nicolaos was in his study, enjoying an afternoon's respite from more pressing labors, perusing the writings of Origen.[30] Hearing someone approach, he looked up to see Arsenios, his father's steward, in the door, red faced and in an obvious state of agitation.

"Forgive the intrusion, young master," the man was saying, "but as a son you will know your duty and will want to fulfill it."

"My duty? What duty is this, sir? Of what are you speaking?"

"They did not want you to know—did not want you to come—for fear of contagion."

"Who, man? Speak plainly!"

"Your parents. They have been very ill, and now I am sure are to the brink of dying."

A stab to the heart, or the sensation of his heart falling, his head of a sudden floating. He managed to say softly, "And I am hearing of this only now."

Arsenios, a Christian, looked regretful to the point of tears and beat his breast. "As I say, they did not want you to know. I did not want to disobey. But I do fear their time is short. I have ordered a cisium[31] to bear you home."

Nicolaos moved quickly. Collecting the holy oils he kept to hand, he moved an arm over Arsenios in a gesture of blessing. "Do not distress yourself,

---

30 Origin of Alexandria, also known as Origin Adamantius, c. 185 – 253 A.D., Christian scholar, ascetic and theologian
31 small chariot for one or two persons

man. Offer the chariot to my uncle. You will find him in the upper rooms. I know the shorter way by foot. I will anoint them, but I must go quickly."

He set out on a run, praying aloud as he went. "Jesus, Lord and brother, be with them! My father, my mother, your servants Phánios and Johanna! Do not allow them to be fearful, please; uphold their faith. I pray you, restore them and let them live, Lord! But thy will be done, not my own." The day was warm, the sun intense; whether from the heat or from his own fear, he found it hard to breathe. Twice he stumbled over loose cobbles and nearly dropped the precious jar of chrism blessed for the remission of sins and for passage to eternal life; yet on he ran, repeating again and again, "Thy will, not mine, Lord."

At last the Patara lighthouse came into view, the first marker of home. He was flushed as with fever, sweat streaming inside his clothing. He willed himself to run faster, his prayer now silent from his bursting heart, for he had no breath left to voice it. "Graces, Lord, from your atoning death, which fulfilled the prophecy of Isaiah, 'He bore our infirmities and endured our sufferings.'[32] Please, please, dear Jesus! Yet not my will, but yours."

Reaching the courtyard, with sounds of grief inside assailing his ears, he stopped a moment on the threshold and leaned on the doorpost, gasping to fill his lungs.

The room was redolent with vinegar, eucalyptus, and tincture of liquid amber. They were in their bed chamber, lying side by side on their backs, uncovered and unclad save for cloths folded across their breasts and hips. Their eyes were closed, their hands entwined as lovers. Their fingers and toes and the tips of their noses were black with decay.[33] They were gone already, at peace. Nicolaos rent his outer garment and cried out to his God, a visceral, agonized wordless cry. He gazed long at the pair who had given him life, at the suffering they had conspired to spare him in death. Finally, his breathing still labored, he gathered himself and opened the jar of oil.

---

32 Matthew 8:17 NAB, paraphrased
33 Necrosis or gangrene resulting from Bubonic plague, *Yersinia pestis*

XIV

The plague, it seemed, had been growing in secret with rapacious speed among the poor near the wharfs of Lycian ports, migrating slowly and less significantly to the inner cities. It would claim countless lives, particularly the very young and the very old, before it burned itself out, decimating households and laying waste to business and trade all along the coast. Indeed, after Nicolaos had seen to the burial of his parents in the crypt below their church, he realized there were at least a dozen people who had depended upon them for their livelihood. They now looked to him; he was the young master no more.

His father's business concerns, the shipping and inter-city commerce, could continue under the direction of Arsenios, who had been trusted by Epiphánios for years and had proven himself worthy. The matter of the property near the lighthouse, however, the family home, grounds and staff, was another matter. As a holy presbyter with an established place within the bishop's inner circle, Nicolaos had no need for a fine house or servants; yet those quarters had history and potential, and the people serving them needed work. It was a burdensome quandary, for a period of time while the death of his parents was a fresh wound in his heart.

Through consultation with Arsenios he learned that his father had kept his sizeable fortune on deposit with a local argentarius[34] and had preferred to maintain it as vacua pecunia,[35] earning no interest but also incapable of being invested on his behalf, for he did not trust the Roman system. Even so,

---

34 banker, moneychanger
35 simple savings

it was an impressive sum, and by right of inheritance it now fell to Nicolaos. The very thought was somewhat overwhelming.

Methodius had reeled under the loss of his sister and her husband, who had truly been a brother. Weeks had passed, but little had changed. He was a few years younger than either Johanna or Phánios, but he was feeling his advanced age now as never before. He began to question the simplest decisions, to doubt the value of his homilies, his writings; to feel unsure of himself for the first time in life. It was uncharacteristic of him to give way to melancholia, if that was what was happening to him, and it was unsettling. Prayer did not give him the solace it once did; he persisted with it, but it did not make him feel closer to God.

Despondent, tired and a little hungry, he descended the stairs in evening darkness and drifted in the direction of his nephew's study, drawn by the light of a single oil lamp. Nicolaos was alone, seated at table, his head in his hands. Hesitant to intrude on a grieving man's weeping, nevertheless he cleared his throat and said, "Sorrow is a heavy burden, my son."

Nicolaos raised his head and with shining eyes declared, "Uncle, I choose joy." He motioned the old man to enter, come closer. "My parents embraced the Eucharist, the 'medicine of immortality,'[36] he said quietly. "They are with Christ Jesus. I choose joy."

Those words harkened back to the day Johanna had come to her brother, fraught with worry about her son. He had asked her, "Has he joy?" Methodius choked back a sob. Nicolaos in his solitude had been praying. It was he himself who was weeping.

---

36 Ignatius of Antioch to the Ephesians, 20:2

"Come, uncle, take heart." Nicolaos rose and put an arm around his shoulders. "Friends have sent gastrin from my mother's kitchen. Shall we share it, with a draught of wine?"

The bishop nodded and went willingly with his nephew. God in His wisdom indeed had touched this young one; the scholar had become the teacher.

XV

Clodio also had agonized through the long weeks that the plague gripped Patara. He witnessed the deaths of his father, his oldest brother, and his younger sister Anika's little daughter, who was not yet walking. Vivienne's mother had suffered terribly with fever, seizures and delirium before she too was taken, about the same time the parents of his good friend Nicolaos were struck down. Nearly everyone in his Christian assembly near the sea had lost someone. The common greeting was no longer, "Good day, friend, peace be with you," but "How many, friend? How many need our prayers today?" And prayer was not all that was needed.

Before Nicolaos sent for him, Clodio had surveyed his visage in a mirror of polished tin and realized that he appeared to have aged years in a matter of weeks. His eyes were sunken and rimmed with gray, his skin overall bore an unhealthy pallor, and his forehead was permanently creased by worry and anguish. There was no help for it. He was surprised, therefore, to find his friend looking much the same as ever he had. His manner was not untouched by sadness, certainly, but Nicolaos was smooth of brow, cool eyed and serene.

He was greeted warmly with an embrace. They were meeting at the family home, the imposing yellow stone house above the lighthouse cliff. Clodio could not help but be overcome with wonder. The spaciousness, the sumptuous furnishings, the servants bringing food and drink, all were novel to him.

"You have not been here before."

"No."

"Mea culpa."[37] Nicolaos said. "In some ways I was more at home at the wharfs and on the beach."

"Aye, Sea Turtle, I remember." Clodio tasted a nut-filled pastry laced with honey. "My mother always marveled at the delicacies your mother sent to us. How she would exclaim to see this place!"

Nicolaos smiled. "Then you have quickly brought us to what has troubled my mind and to what I propose."

"Indeed?"

"I have inherited all this"—he swept his hand about him—"all my father's property, all of his business dealings."

Clodio nodded.

"I have no need of it."

Clodio slowly nodded again, but was puzzled.

"I wish to give this house to you."

He was stunned, dumfounded, but in an instant began to find words. "I cannot! This is too great a gift! I must earn what I—"

Nicolaos held up a hand to stay him. "Hear me out. There is space enough here for your family, your honored mother, even a workshop for you, should you wish it. But there are many rooms, Clodio, in my father's house"—he grinned, enjoying the unintended parallel to Scripture—"and there are folk here used to service; like you, they need to earn their bread."

"I'm listening."

"So many good people in our city of Patara have lost so much; you know this. Widows, orphans. Some can care for themselves, but others cannot. Some need only a helping hand; others need love and care."

Clodio felt his soul soaring, for he surmised what was coming. Never had he loved his friend more.

"If I give you charge of this place, will you open its doors and share it?"

---

37 my fault

"You know that I will!"

They embraced again, and their laughter set the birds in the courtyard to singing.

✠

Two full months passed before the friends saw each other again. This time Nicolaos was the honored guest at the great yellow stone house above the lighthouse cliff. Clodio was his eager host, and Vivienne, fresh, lovely, and quite at ease in her role, was hostess. Homemaking became her; still the bride, her pale hair curled in soft tendrils around her face, which seemed to glow. She could not contain her pleasure, serving the men with foods she herself had prepared, then joining them at table. Nicolaos was glad to see the Greek custom of female subservience was no longer practiced within these walls. It had often made him feel uncomfortable to see his mother wait to eat the leavings of men, although she had accepted the practice as right and natural.

Their experiment in charity was a resounding success, Clodio told him. Two widows and their small children, as well as three unrelated youths orphaned by plague, had taken up residence; and all were agreed there was room enough for a few more unfortunates. The three youths were learning the woodworking trade in Clodio's workshop. The eldest of them, who was educated but penniless, also served as tutor for the children. The two widows were eager to help with the upkeep of the household and with the cooking.

"But Vivienne did all the cooking for this feast," Clodio said proudly, pleased to see her color with humility.

And feast it was: Sliced boiled quail eggs with fennel, whitefish lightly charred with oregano and bathed in olive oil, lentils with onions, a soft goat cheese and stewed figs. The bread for sopping was unleavened yet light, with an excellent nutlike flavor.

"Vivienne, this is a meal for kings!"

She colored the more and cast down her eyes with modesty.

After the meal Vivienne cleared the dishes from the table and left the men alone, but not before gesturing significantly to her husband.

When she was gone Clodio confided, "My good wife will present me with a son—or a daughter—in the spring of the year." He was flushed with pride.

"God be praised!"

"And before you take leave of us, she wishes that I bring an important matter to your attention."

"I am all ears," said Nicolaos.

"She has a friend—this girl and her two sisters attended the wedding. Unremarkable, but you might recall them. Dark haired maidens, none too lean but still fine to look upon, close in age and each like the other."

"Aye?"

"They are the daughters of the barrel maker your father dealt with, in the commerce district near the public wharfs."

Nicolaos nodded. "Old Demetrios. I know the business and the house. But was there not a fire at the barrel yard?"

"Exactly. And the mother of the girls was taken by the plague. The father lives, but his lungs are weak, his business is gone, and in his grief he has turned to strong wine and betting on the races."[38]

"And has backed the wrong faction, no doubt."

"Every time. The youngest daughter was dowerless to begin, but now the elder two have none. We at the Christian assembly have offered to help the man, but he is proud and angry and will not hear of it."

"I see."

---

38 chariot races, normally featuring four sponsored "factions" of one to three chariots each

"He cannot provide for his daughters. The rumor is that he plans to sell them."

Nicolaos hung his head for a moment. That would mean a life of harlotry for three innocent children of God.

"Of course my Vivienne is distraught with worry for them," Clodio added.

"As well she would be."

"We are praying for a better outcome."

Nicolaos smiled at his good hearted friend. "Leave it with me," he said.

XVI

Night had fallen without and was steadily creeping within. The one candle lighting the little room was about to gutter, and the cook fire had subsided to embers. They had left him a large chunk of barley bread and a generous portion of the beans, cooked and recooked until they were mush. His girls were too good to him, Demetrios reflected, far better than he deserved. He had the warmth of wine in his belly and reasoned that he needed no more than that; yet the beans would dry and spoil and the bread would mold, if left overnight. So he pulled the food on the hearth closer to him and began to eat, tasting his shame.

How he missed the righteousness of a day's hard work, the triumph of a living earned by skill and honest dealings. How he missed his good wife, who always had a wise word for him, whose breast was a willing pillow for his weary head! They would pray together of an evening like this, singing psalms to the girls and offering praises. But she was gone, his girls were doomed and he would soon die a failure. Of what use was prayer now?

Nevertheless, "Help me, Lord," he wheezed in the growing dark. The wheeze became a cough, and the cough a racking spasm. "Help me."

Chink! He heard a sound in the corner under the open window, as though something had fallen. He thought he could dimly see an object on the floor.

Setting his plate aside, he moved to the corner and picked up a leather pouch laden with something heavy. Bringing it to the candlelight, he drew the string and spilled out onto the table a handful of golden coins. Roman Aureus glinting in splendor, enough for a dowry, enough for a wedding, and more! He rubbed his eyes, he bit down on a coin—real, as real as any he had ever encountered—and he raised his eyes heavenward in awe.

And so it transpired that his eldest daughter was wed in the Christian church by the sea, with her sisters and friend Vivienne in attendance. There was much rejoicing, and Demetrios thanked God for the blessing. He hardly had time to begin to worry over the remaining two dowerless girls at home when—chink!—another pouch of gold coins was tossed through his window in the dark of night. He rushed to the door hoping to see his benefactor, but no one was there.

In a short time there was a second wedding, God be praised, and only one child left to provide for. Could he dare hope? He began to pray that his patron be revealed to him, if only so that he might remember such a generous soul in prayer. Keeping his sandals on and sleeping near the door, he kept watch as best he could each night until he heard the third gift drop into the room.

Demetrios moved more quickly than he had thought possible and dimly saw a figure hurrying away. Running, he managed to catch the man's cloak.

"Wait! Please!"

The man turned toward him and stepped from the shadows. He knew this face! "Young master," he exclaimed. "No! No longer that, your honor, but I do know you! You are the son of Epiphánios, now a holy priest!"

"Peace be upon you, friend," Nicolaos said. "What need have you of me?"

Demetrios let go the cloak, feeling suddenly humbled. "I wish only to thank you, sir. And to ask you why."

Nicolaos looked kindly on him. "Because our father God through his Son commanded that we love one another, and because I knew that as a father you would use the gifts wisely."

Demetrios was moved to tears. "You must have the seat of honor at the next wedding," he said.

"No, please. Tell no one of this, for the Lord also said that we should do our good deeds in secret."

The old man nodded.

"Pray for me," Nicolaos said. "That will be enough."

And so they parted, both uplifted and grateful to God, one for kindness received, and one for the means to be kind. But truth has its own way of finding the light. In time the story of holy Nicolaos, secret gift giver, would become well known among men.

XVII

As time wore on Nicolaos felt himself in the grip of a strange dilemma. The more his ministry prospered, the farther he felt from God. The more well-known he became and the more he was sought out, the more he wished for obscurity. He began to yearn for a return to the quiet contemplative life that had come so naturally to him before he was made a presbyter. He felt somewhat guilty about that, but the call was undeniable.

"Uncle, do you not feel that our ministry intrudes on our own piety? Are we not drawn away from peace and into the affairs of the world by the demands placed upon us?"

Nicolaos was in earnest, flushed with embarrassment. Methodius pulled on his beard as he formulated an answer. Imparting wisdom was precarious.

"Jesus Christ was God," he said, "yet he took the role of servant; service is what is asked of us." Seeing his nephew was close to tears, he added tenderly, "All of us. Not only presbyters, deacons and bishops. All of us who follow him are asked to love and serve one another, and in so doing, to spread his Word."

"I know that. I know it in my head, but my heart longs . . ."

"For the purity of solitude?"

"Yes." His eyes widened; clearly, he was a little surprised at being understood.

"The great Irenaeus said, 'God did not tell us to follow him because he needed our help, but because he knew that loving him would make us whole.'"[39]

---

39 St. Irenaeus of Lyons, Greek bishop from Smyrna in Anatolia

"Yes, Uncle."

Methodius did not like to see his nephew downcast. "Sometimes the very thing we seek to avoid is the thing which brings us closer to what we need."

"Uncle?"

"I think perhaps you must bestir yourself, step into the tide of life, meet others where they strive and live, and in that strange and utter chaos find your inner peace." Nicolaos looked bewildered. Obviously the lad did not understand. He must speak more plainly. "It would benefit you, Nicolaos, to leave Patara, where you are grounded, and to seek out others of our faith in the land where The Way began. To walk in the footsteps of our Lord."

"The Holy Land!" Nicolaos exclaimed in hushed tones.

"Aye. I myself have been as far as Antioch, Ephesus and Patmos, where the apostles lived and taught. But to see Judea—to walk upon paths where Christ walked—that would be a balm to me, were I not too old to travel so far."

"The Holy Land!"

"You may make ready for the spring of the year, if you wish. Your good steward Arsenios will be able to arrange safe passage, I should think."

"But Uncle, am I not needed here with you?"

Methodius smiled inside, to hear himself perceived in terms of obligation. "I have presbyters enough, and sufficient deacons, and the good Deaconess Mena. You will be missed, nephew, but the work will advance. You will go with my blessing."

The Holy Land!

"Did I not tell you, Sea Turtle? Did I not say you would see the world?" Clodio was beside himself with glee. He was fairly dancing where he stood, and grinning from ear to ear.

"You said I would go far and see amazing things," Nicolaos recalled. "I only wish I could take you with me!"

"Ah, but this scorpion is happy to remain on this land, with all that is his own about him." His face fell suddenly. "You will be here for the birth?"

"Of course I will. And the baptism!"

They were seated once more on the public wharf within sight of the lighthouse, watching the ships on the water and the scudding clouds and the birds in the sky, just as in the old days.

"I will not leave until the late spring of the year," Nicolaos assured his friend, "when the snows will be gone from the mountains, the sun will be strong, mare clausum[40] will be over, and the sea will be restful."

The Patera Lighthouse

_____

40 navigation downtime, during the winter months

XVIII

The sea will be restful.

Nicolaos stood on the pitching deck of the vessel that would take him from Myra to Caesarea Maritima[41] and wondered at his naivety. All his life he had loved the notion of seafaring, had ascribed to a romantic concept that, he realized now, had little in common with reality. The long overland trip from Patara to Myra had been tedious, most of it over rough terrain; but the rocking of the raeda[42] and the lumbering of its oxen had not prepared him for the constant roll of the sea. That motion, coupled with the combination of smells on the afterdeck—unwashed bodies, night soil, the accursed Roman garum[43]—kept his stomach in a state of unrest and drew him to the relief of the corbita's bow and its flow of fresh sea air. He could have asked Arsenios to secure him a place below deck in either of the two cargo holds with the amphorae[44] and grain sacks, but he had deemed that type of accommodation an unusual, unnecessary expense. And surely the closeness of such an arrangement below would have proven as taxing as the tented passenger spaces on deck.

His uncle had been right, of course. He needed to experience more of the world, more of the life common to others unlike himself. To this end he had at first welcomed an association with a Greek already aboard from Corinth on business—much of the amphorae and other pottery in the hold were his—and

---

41 capital of the Roman Province Syria Palaestina in Judea; today, Caesarea, Israel
42 four-wheeled wagon with benches
43 popular sauce of fermented fish intestines
44 storage jars

with a friendly Pataran sailor named Georgios whom he remembered from his youth as one of his father's men who had encouraged his shipboard visits.

The Greek, called Cosmas, was a Stoic fond of debate. He was traveling with his tall and slender Nubian slave, who attended him with a fervor that could only come from fear. With very little gray hair, wide set gray eyes beneath thin arched brows and with a jutting, clean shaven chin, his face— particularly in profile— presented Cosmas as an aloof and sternly impassive individual. Nicolaos wondered how the principle of equality in nature which was so celebrated in Stoicism could support the enslavement of another human being.

After two days of philosophical contest—try as Nicolaos might to avoid it—Cosmas had clearly recognized a challenging intellectual adversary and thus had continued to seek out the lone presbyter with relentless precision. Aside from his loudly proclaimed opinions, Cosmas cut quite the figure among the few other passengers, who were clearly Christian pilgrims or unassuming men of commerce. He made a great show of possession of a bright rose colored cloak of oiled silk which protected him from chill and spray when the corbita's full sails thrust the ship forward, but could be whipped off for comfort when less speed was achieved or when the sun was high and blazing. His slave followed at his elbow, eyes lowered in servitude, keeping employed with the cloak and the carrying of a water flask.

"You think that I am not educated in this Christian Way you follow."

"I make no assumptions."

"The universe is god, and the Logos[45] manifests in breath of fire, not unlike your Holy Spirit."

Nicolaos shook his head. "God made the universe. My Father God the creator is one with his Son Jesus, and with the Holy Spirit."

"You deny that the Logos is within nature?"

45 in classical Greek and neo-Platonic philosophy, the cosmic reason giving order, purpose and intelligibility to the world

"Nature is also God's work," Nicolaos said. "What I deny, as you put it, is that God is merely ephemeral, like the wind in these sails above us."

The Nubian's attention was darting from one to the other; clearly he was unused to any challenge of his master's statements.

"God is the author of all life," Nicolaos continued, "all we can see and all we cannot see. He was, before his creation of this world; he exists presently, in the now; he ever shall be, beyond time as we know it. His Son lived among men and gave up his human life for all men, to atone for their sinfulness. He is my brother. The Holy Spirit is my advocate, my guide, my consoler. And yet the three are one."

The Stoic was scowling, the slave enthralled. From his watch post Georgios listened closely.

"Surely if you have studied The Way you can grasp the difference between Stoicism and Christianity," Nicolaos observed gently.

"I have found your beliefs to be unproved and against logic," Cosmas declared. "I must follow where common reason leads, without passion. I must strive to live in harmony with nature and the virtues of wisdom, courage, justice and temperance."

"On that we can agree," Nicolaos smiled. "I ask the Holy Spirit for such graces every day."

The two men drifted away from Nicolaos, the slave glancing back as he trailed his master.

The hazy sun was setting over the stern of the ship, casting a sickly pale light on the tents and reclining bodies huddled there. Nicolaos decided he would remain in the bow alone, nestled in the shadow cast by the artemon[46] mast and its outcroppings. He drew chunks of bread and cheese and a fistful of pressed dates from his provisions bag and asked a blessing on the food that would nourish him until morning.

The good Bishop Methodius has been right about many things, Nicolaos admitted to himself. He would not be much missed in Patara. There were deacons and presbyters enough to carry on the work of the several Christian assemblies within his uncle's purview, and the young Deaconess Mena had proven to be an invaluable help, particularly with the women among them. They would fare perfectly well without him. And if he could not reach the mind of an educated man such as Cosmas, of what effect would all the rest of his ministry be?

The wind was quickening. The stars might not appear tonight to inspire his prayers with their beauty, for the sky had been heavily overcast all day. He would pray nonetheless, adding Cosmas and his servant to the souls for whom he felt responsible; and confident in the goodness of God, undoubtedly he would eventually sleep well.

---

46 headsail

XIX

Georgios trembled whenever he recalled the events of the next day. How, when they were well south of the Cyprus Island, the morning broke more like twilight than dawn. How the clouds that roiled and darkened hid the rising sun, heralding the violent storm that was so fearful, a foul black squall. How they feared for their ship, for their very lives. And how sudden the light and warmth came, overwhelming and breathtaking, when the weather cleared.

He had not recognized the young master when first he boarded in Myra. A man he was now, sturdy grown, a handsome man with full lips, a strong chin, high forehead and kind brown eyes; familiar somehow. But when he spoke, aye, when he spoke in that deep mellow timbre, and the manner of his speaking, so calm and sympathetic like, aye, he knew him then. More than civil he was, no owner's airs, but friendly as an old shipmate.

The young master had spent the night on the foredeck by the foremast with a mantle pulled over him, keeping himself to himself and troubling no one. The pinch-faced Greek who had made it his business to pester and prod him since he had boarded had bedded near the tenting and the other passengers, yet well apart, nearer to the foredeck, with his black slave at his feet. And he, Georgios, had just resumed the morning watch.

The squall broke with a sudden and intense fury. For a dozen years or more Georgios had sailed these waters, to and fro with the merchantmen. He understood the tides, knew the deeps, the shoals, the pull of the waves when weather hit, like he knew his woman in the dark. But when that first shaft of lightning plunged, a spear from on high, its thunder-voice cracking close on, he was a boy again, quaking and clinging to the rail like a landsman, his heart thudding in his chest. Thrice the ship rode sickeningly high for a moment, then fell all awash, as the whipping rain pelted and hail bounced like pebbles on the deck. There was shouting from the crew, shrieks and turmoil aft as tents ripped and tore loose. The Greek's red cloak took flight on the wind, landing on the breast of the sea like a bloodstain, then was gone. The old Greek's mouth had gone slack with fear, and his black slave's eyes were big as bird's eggs.

It was after the third perilous rise and shuddering fall, the ship canting to a degree that had passengers and crew alike scrambling and wailing, that the young master stood up. Bracing against the foremast, he lifted face and arms to the downpour. Despite the din Georgios heard every word from the young master's mouth, and he was sure the Greek and his man did also: "My Jesus, you stayed the storm on Galilee! Have mercy on us, Lord, send your peace!"

The swiftness of the halt of rain and punishing wind, the speed with which the clouds parted, and the quick drying heat of the low hanging sun was near as frightening as the storm had been. It was like a miracle. Georgios would not soon forget it. Nay, he would never forget.

A handsome man with full lips, a strong chin, high forehead
and kind brown eyes

XX

The Stoic was noticeably subdued, neither moving conspicuously about the deck as he had done before the storm, nor seeking conversation. Nicolaos was glad of the respite and welcomed the opportunity to commune with his Lord Jesus in relative privacy. The prayer shouted in rain and wind had been answered so quickly, so dramatically, that he himself was awed and moved to thoughtful reflection. For perhaps the first time he believed without hesitation born of self-doubt that through God all things were possible; that he might offer himself where needed as an instrument of the Almighty. He thought of the blessing of his Nonna, now a vague and dreamlike memory, yet somehow surely the lodestone at the heart of his faith. He thought of his friend Clodio, truly a gift from God, and the love in his eyes when asked at his son's baptism how the child shall be called. Looking to his wife for confirmation readily given with a nod, "His name is Nicolaos," his friend had declared proudly. And he thought of his parents in the tomb, that their entry into eternity must be like this; after the dimness and strife of life on earth, the brilliance of light and warmth and joy.

The sea remained calm in dazzling blue perfection after the tempest had subsided; the warm winds were favorable and steady. In less than two days' time the white stone walls and towers of Caesarea Maritima appeared on the horizon, glistening in the sun like distant snowcaps. Nicolaos watched with admiration as the crew eased the corbita into and through the manmade Sebastos[47] Harbor. And what a harbor it was! Built by Herod the Great for

---

47 *Sebastos* is Greek for *Augustus*; the harbor was dedicated to Caesar Augustus about 10 B.C.

Rome and for glory, it was said to rival the port of Athens; that 300 ships could be accommodated here. Its vastness put the anchorages of Lycia to shame. It was here in Caesarea by the sea that the Apostle Peter baptized Cornelius the centurion and his household, conferring for the first time Christian baptism upon Gentiles. It was here that Phillip the Deacon bestowed hospitality upon Paul the Apostle during his missionary journeys; and here that Paul was imprisoned for two years before being transported to Rome. All this history Nicolaos knew just as he knew his own, and this wealth of knowledge added to his elation at landing in Palestine.

He took leave of his fellow passengers, wishing them fruitful pilgrimage or profitable business, thanked the able crew, and embraced Georgios. Gazing back, he saw the Greek's Nubian slave wistfully looking after him. He raised a hand, and the man flashed a smile, holding his own hand high in the air for as long as Nicolaos could see.

His legs were still adjusting to the unyielding ground, a firmness so welcome yet so oddly strange after the voyage, when a dark young man with a genial Semitic visage beneath a white shawl stepped forward to present him with a walking staff and a flagon of wine. "I am Abram," he said, "Welcome, friend."

XXI

"I will be your guide; your companion, should you wish it," Abram said. "Your Bishop Methodius has asked this of my bishop, Theotecnus of Caesarea, and I am most happy to be of service." He made a rather stately bow.

Nicolaos was astonished; this was unexpected. He gazed about himself, somewhat overwhelmed by the size of this city on the Sharon plain.[48] There were buildings, both tall and sprawling, as far as the eye could see in every direction save the sea at his back, and the whole of the scene seemed to be teeming with activity. From the wharf he could see the graduated rise of an amphitheater, filling with people even at this rather early hour; cobbled streets beside it spilling out carts and chariots. He could hear loud market cries, the fevered calls of commerce, from a steaming and odorous seaside enclave. And everywhere upon the vast metropolis, the mark of Rome.

"I shall be grateful," Nicolaos said. "I did not know of my bishop's request, but as I am familiar with his wisdom, I should have guessed."

Abram's swarthy face split with a wide grin of satisfaction. "Excellent!" he exclaimed. "Come! We shall begin with a prayer and a meal. There are tabernae[49] in Caesarea aplenty, but in such establishments one is beset by whores and thieves anxious to part one from his money as he sleeps, or later when accosted on the road. You will be safe in my home, and my good wife will ply you as a wayward son come home—that is to say, she will feed you well!"

---

48 once the largest city in Judea, with an estimated population of 125,000 over an urban area of 1.4 square miles; now ruins, part of an Israeli national park
49 inns

✠

Abram's wife Miriam was as good as his word. She was kindly, respect-ful of his station as a presbyter, and much concerned for his comfort. A basin and urn of clean water were provided for washing the moment he crossed her threshold. "You are thin," she clucked disapprovingly. "You must be famished and tired after so many days at sea! No fresh foods, no fixed place to lay your head."

"I will not deny it."

"Then put off thy shoes and recline here in the cool; my daughters and I will see you nourished. Husband, your sandals!"

Abram winked at his guest, obediently removed his footwear and settled himself on cushions as his wife and two giggling young girls set before them a small feast—roast lamb and charred fish, aromatic grains, cucumbers in brine, grapes, olives, and a wonderful salty cheese that crumbled on the tongue.

"This is very fine, truly," Nicolaos said. The herbed wine also was light and most flavorful.

Miriam nodded in humble acknowledgment, bringing a plate of unleav-ened bread and boiled figs at the last. Taking a seat herself off to one side, she folded her arms across her ample breast and beamed with satisfaction. She was rather like her husband, sunburned and bright eyed.

"My instructions are to assist you in any endeavor," Abram began. "I believe you wish to walk the ministry of Our Lord."

"That's right, I would like to visit the places He knew, as much as I can."

"God be praised," Miriam murmured, still smiling.

"I am sure you know," Abram said, "that the Jerusalem of the time of Christ is no more. All in Judea is changed, thanks to the rule of Rome. Even this capital, Caesarea Maritima, so named since Our Lord's day in King Herod's time, is now properly called Caesarea Palestinae."

"Words, words," murmured Miriam, shaking her head, no longer smiling.

"There are fewer and fewer Jews here in Caesarea; our population is mostly pagan."

"Godless devils," muttered Miriam.

"Woman! Allow me to speak."

Lifting her chin defiantly, "I wish you to speak. Tell him about Jerusalem!"

"I will come to that. The Way of the Lord has a small but strong community in the city; many house churches, two with the history of Phillip and Origen within them.[50] And we have here a theology school with a great library, perhaps the best in all the world." Abram cast a cautionary gaze toward his wife. She wore a neutral expression and remained silent. "But of course all goes forward under the watchful eye of Rome. We are not encouraged."

"It is much the same in Lycia," Nicolaos offered.

"Jerusalem was destroyed, as you will know—pulled down, looted, defiled and burned—generations ago.[51] But what you may not know is that all that remains of the Second Holy Temple of Jehovah is part of a retaining wall that supported the slope of the temple mount. A shrine to Jupiter stands in its place. Even the name was wiped away; the city, which is yet rebuilding, is called Aelia Capitolina. On the hill where Our Lord was crucified there is now a temple dedicated to the Roman goddess Venus. Jews are not allowed entry into the city that was Jerusalem, save for one day a year, the Tisha B'Av, when they mourn the destruction of their temples and the Holy of Holies. Most of the Christians in Judea have Jewish heritage, as we do"—glancing at his wife, who nodded—"so it follows that Christians are not welcome there."

"And Bethlehem?" Nicolaos asked.

"Gone. The cave where the Lord Jesus was said to be born is covered by a temple to Adonis."

---

50 Origen Adimantius was founder of the Christian School at Caesarea
51 70 A.D., the Siege of Jerusalem in the first Jewish-Roman War, under Titus, later Emperor of Rome

A deep sigh from Miriam.

"Then tell me what I may see," Nicolaos said softly.

Abram brightened. "We will go north," he said. "The longest distance is the first, to Nazareth. We may hire a raeda and stop at tabernae, or we may go afoot and stay with friends of The Way two nights on the road."

"Oh, assuredly by foot, if you are agreeable."

"Agreeable? I have prayed for no less!" Abram exclaimed. "The opportunity to explore Galilean hospitality is a treasure from the Lord! Our brothers in The Way shall show us every courtesy."

"As will our sisters," said Miriam, smiling again.

"Nazareth is still a Jewish village, where Christians live peaceably among the Jews, in mutual respect. There we will see the house where Mary, the mother of Our Lord, lived when the angel came to her. The place, it is said, where Joseph and Jesus worked with adz and saw to earn their bread. Their synagogue, where the Lord preached that the Scripture was fulfilled in him, and the Qafza cliff where his neighbors would have thrown him to his death for the saying of it."

"My husband is a learned man," Miriam said proudly.

"Hush, woman!"

"I am sure she speaks the truth," said Nicolaos.

Barely concealing his pleasure, Abram cleared his throat and went on. "From Nazareth, Cana is an easy walk, half a day, no more. And it was there that Jesus performed his first sign."

"Water into wine," whispered his wife, pouring more of their own libation.

They each sipped from their cups, as though in silent toast to the first of many miracles.

"From Cana," Abram said, "on to Capernaum, and perhaps to Magdala, both of them on the Sea of Galilee."

"And my husband, shall you take him to the Agape?"

Abram sat back on his haunches, considering. "If our guest desires it." He appeared lost in thought for a moment. "You have heard of the holy hermits?"

"Yes."

"There are those who stay in the desert and deny themselves the pleasures of life among other men. They deny themselves everything but prayer." He shrugged slightly. "We have such a one in Galilee, in a cave in the hills where the Baptist lived. His name is Linus of Antioch, but they call him Agape, which means—"

"The love of God," said Nicolaos.

"Aye. And among those who have sought him out, he is called that. Simply that."

XXII

They set out on their journey at first light the next morning. Miriam brought her guest a square of white linen to cover his head, similar to the shawl that Abram wore. "It will cool you when the sun is high," she said. Nicolaos kept his travel bag with him. Miriam outfitted each of them further with a wineskin, a water flask, and a canvas bag filled with unleavened bread, dried fruit, nuts and cheese. "For your strength." She stood in the dooryard flanked by her little girls, watching as the men strode away, and chanting a blessing prayer for safe return.

It took them more than an hour's walk simply to be clear of the city. Great white marble buildings finally gave way to the simple structures of piled gray basalt and pale limestone common to the countryside of Samarian Judea. Far beyond the Roman-built aqueduct and wide cobbled roads lined with cypress, their well-trodden path of packed sand became only slightly less wide but much more comfortable beneath their sandals. The vegetation north of Caesarea was green and lush and splashed with the color of wildflowers, blue thistles, irises, and pinks he was told were lilies. "The lilies of the field," Nicolaos thought, and felt a lightness in his step with the joy of their beauty.

Their first evening was spent with fellow travelers, many of them Christians, at a way-side shelter adjacent a well in the midst of a grove of date palms. A family known to Abram fed them and made them welcome that night, refusing all payment but prayer.

Because the second morning was the Lord's Day, Nicolaos lay his white head cloth upon a flat stone near the wayside shelter, pulled a tiny olive-wood cross, an agate cup and a plate from his travel bag and thus shared the Eucharist with their host family and fellow believers, consecrating the wine and bread Miriam had provided. There were perhaps thirteen men and women, and several children gathered there.

"We offer to you the bread and the cup, yielding you thanks, because you have counted us worthy to stand before you and to minister to you. And we pray that you would send your Holy Spirit upon the offering of your holy Church; that you, gathering them into one, would grant to all your saints who partake to be filled with the Holy Spirit, that their faith may be confirmed in truth, that we may praise and glorify you. Through your Servant Jesus Christ, through whom be to you glory and honor, with the Holy Spirit, in the holy Church, both now and always and world without end. Amen."[52]

Nicolaos spoke to the small crowd with an easy affection, expounding on parables of the Lord in that strong deep voice that was simultaneously warm and gentle. Abram was well pleased with his illustrious charge and felt an unseemly pride in accompanying him. "It is well, is it not," he said to the assembly, "to set the Lord's Table under the open sky?"

Nicolaos responded for all: "It is well, indeed. God's green land is the finest church, and the birds of the air the ablest choir."

One of the children present gleefully clapped his hands at this; Abram frowned and his mother began to rebuke him.

"Nay, the child is right," Nicolaos told her. "We must all remember to applaud God's goodness and to thank him daily for the simple splendor of his creation." He took the dried grapes and walnuts from his canvas bag and gave them to the children. Feeling abashed, Abram did the same, but later along the road remarked that, owing to the holy breaking of the bread and their generosity to the young, they now had naught to eat.

"God will provide," his companion said. And God did.

---

52 from the Canon of Hippolytus of Rome (c. 170 A.D. – c. 235 A.D.)

XXIII

A steady pace brought them that afternoon to flowing water, a deep river that was narrow as a brook in places; and across one of those narrow stretches a manmade bridge of stepping stones and hewn timbers invited them to cross in safety. The sun danced on the water beneath them, its reflection like so many traveling diamonds. "The Kishon," Abram informed him. "It means 'the gifted river.'"

"I like the name," Nicolaos said. "Gifted with life and refreshment for many." They stopped on the far bank to refill their flasks. "But what is that sound?"

"Water on the rocks. It is much more rapid below here."

"No, there is something else."

He followed the faint mewling sound to a crevice in the embankment, half hidden by reeds and undergrowth. Something gray and ivory was wedged there, exhausted from struggling.

"Abram! Come quickly! A goat!"

It was a young doe, swollen with milk, whose rear left leg was caught between rocks.

"Hold her," Abram said. He worked her leg free and washed grit and blood from the scraped place with water from his flask. "They are nimble creatures, but even they may stumble upon misfortune." He felt the limb with his fingers. "Not broken, then. Suffering more, I think, from her burden."

Nicolaos continued to hold the doe while Abram drew a cup from the bag on his shoulder and deftly relieved her of some of her milk. "I have not always lived in the city," he confided.

They set the goat down on higher ground. She scrambled up the embankment. "Go, find your kids," Abram called after her.

They shared the cup of milk and ate the last of their cheese.

Within an hour's walk from the river they came upon a well-tended vineyard with several rows of early grapes.

"My mother's favorite in the spring," Nicolaos exclaimed. "Green, yet ripe and sweet." While Abram looked on in dismay, Nicolaos helped himself to several clusters, tasted and smiled with satisfaction. "Here. Take, eat."

Seeing that his guide hesitated, he quoted from memory: "'When you enter the vineyard of your neighbor you may eat as many grapes as you please, but you must not take away any in a basket.'"

"The Book of Leviticus?"

"Deuteronomy."[53]

"I knew that," Abram said, tasting his share.

Nicolaos grinned. "I have always lived in the Scriptures."

Thus restored, they pressed on until nightfall. They spent the night conversing and resting beneath olive trees, hardly sated in their stomachs but surely satisfied in their hearts.

---

53 Deuteronomy 23:25 NAB, paraphrased

"I am blessed to be here," Nicolaos said aloud to the darkness, after a long silence. He fervently wished that Clodio were here, to see all that he saw. But as Clodio could not be, he knew he was blessed to have Abram with him.

"Peace be upon you," his companion responded weakly, before falling into a snoring sleep.

Their sunrise walk brought them to the edge of the village of Nazareth, where friends of The Way said to be descended from family of the Lord welcomed them into a house church, with rejoicing and singing of hymns. And much to their delight, feted them with a delicious breakfast.

XXIV

Nicolaos tarried in Nazareth, finding his surroundings fascinating and his hosts most graciously accommodating. There were priestly Jews and there were devout Christians who traced their ancestry to the house of Joseph and the lineage of Mary, and both factions celebrated their connection and were eager to share their knowledge. Listening to their stories, partaking of their hospitality, one was transported to the time of Christ. Visiting the temple of the Lord's earthly father and of his own youth, touching the stones and the very timbers the Lord himself had touched, Nicolaos was brought closer to the reality of Jesus than he could ever have imagined at home in Lycia. He had always walked with God, but here he felt his presence as never before.

After the fifth satisfying day he and Abram left for Cana, bypassing the city of Sepphoris which was so heavily under Roman influence. At Cana they were greeted by the owner of an olive press, who proudly showed off his holdings, the ancient groves, the rows of large amphorae under roof, the donkey press that in harvest season would yield much oil. Oil for the temple in the first press, oil for the table in the second, and oil for lamps in the last. He was a prosperous Jew with a bright eye and a dark beard that descended his chest to two well-groomed points. He seemed effusively anxious to extend hospitality. As he explained, the Christians in Nazareth and Cana and even in Sepphoris were good customers. "Many pilgrims come here," he said knowingly, "for the story of water made wine." He observed his guests closely. "You are making the trek to Arbel?"

"Aye," said Abram. "We will visit the Arbel Valley, Capernaum and Mount Arbel."

"And will you go into the hills, to the Agape?"

Abram could not conceal his surprise. "You know of the Agape?"

The olive grower placed a fingertip aside his nose. "We Jews invented wisdom, my friend. Of course I know of the Agape. My wife carries pickled eggs to him, or rather, she gives them to her sister to deliver; her sister is a Christian."

"I have wondered how he fared in such things."

"The people see that he does not starve. He is well revered."

Nicolaos listened to this exchange with great interest. He had heard of course of the holy hermits of the desert in Egypt, and had wondered about their importance to The Way. Surely each man creates his own inner desert in which to dwell with God, he thought. Yet it would be helpful to learn from such a one who was living his ascetic faith in this historic land.

It was at the height of day after the sun had left its zenith when they left Cana and struck out for the forest and cliffs, in the direction they were told would take them to the Agape. Before leaving the outskirts of the village Nicolaos bought a flagon of herbed wine and some barley bread. "It will be well to take a gift," he said.

They followed a footpath of twists and forks that took them deeper and higher into the wilds; branches and brambles clutched at their garments at every turn. It was late in the day when finally, at a juncture in the path beside a gnarled old plane tree they found a piece of slate upon which the symbol of the fish had been scratched; and a strip of faded blue linen dangled from an upper branch of the tree.

"Here," Abram exclaimed. "This is the sign."

They turned and continued up an incline that was little more than a goat trace, a trail that brought them at last to a ledge in the cliff side and a small cave opening. A soft masculine voice carried to them on the still air: ". . . walk through the valley of the shadow of death, I shall fear no evil."

They found him just inside the aperture, half in light and half in shadow, seated with his legs drawn up beneath him, his hands pressed together in prayer. There was a pervasive odor emanating from the cave, not dank or foul or offensive as one might expect from a space that had long housed a human being in close confines, but sweet; and not a cloying or decaying sweetness, but like the fragrance of flowers and incense combined.

The man had Grecian features but his sunburned skin was dark as that of any Semite; his cheeks, hollow and lined, his brow furrowed. His graying hair was long and straggled, his beard wild. At a muted "Amen," he opened pale eyes that bespoke innocence and humility. They seemed to widen, to start with something like recognition, when they beheld Nicolaos. "Peace be upon you," he said. "A peace surpassing all you have known; the peace of the living God."

"And upon you, brother," Nicolaos said. "Do I address Linus of Antioch?"

The man inclined his head.

"I am Nicolaos of Patera."

"For now," was the strange response.

"And I am Abram, Agape. I bring greetings from the Bishop of Caesarea. We have met before. It was many years ago."

Another nod of the head.

They presented their gifts, the wine and bread. The Agape stirred himself to move somewhat deeper into the cave, creating a space for three and enveloping himself completely in shadow. Even close to the edge of the opening in the rock, the air was cool. There were rugs and faded tapestries spread on the floor of stone, yet it was no seat of comfort.

"You are seeking much?" Although he could not see the Agape's eyes, Nicolaos knew this was directed at him.

"Much, brother." He considered for a moment. "Knowledge. Perhaps assurances."

"There are no assurances beyond the promises of Christ. Be one with him in perfect love and keep his Word, and you will not know death. For he said, 'If anyone keeps this light of mine, he will never see darkness.'[54] Do you believe this to be true, Nicolaos of Patera?"

"I do."

"Then you have knowledge." A moment of silence. "You are consecrated, are you not?"

"Yes, I am a presbyter." Nicolaos wondered how the Agape could know this.

"Then you have perfect love."

Abram exhaled heavily and whispered "Amen."

"We are closest to Christ when through our suffering we share in his cross. Have you found your cross, Nicolaos?"

Nicolaos hesitated. "My faith is a blessing," he said. "There are sacrifices, but I carry no cross."

"It will come."

Abram whistled softly through his teeth. Nicolaos nudged him quiet. "What other words have you for me, Agape?"

He sensed that the holy man was smiling. "The Lord loves a cheerful giver. And you, Nicolaos, have a giving nature, which is not without its own reward. You have within you the capacity for greatness in the eyes of men. Although you will be exalted, take care that you give of yourself with true

---

54 John 8:12 NAB, paraphrased

charity and from humility. 'Humble yourself the more, the greater you are, and you will find favor with God.'"[55]

Silence again. The Agape appeared to be finished. "Those are good words," Abram said. "The hour is late, holy one." The light outside was beginning to fade, and they had brought no torch to help them down the cliff side. "Will you give us your blessing?"

The darkness inside the cave too was deepening. They felt, rather than saw, his hands gentle upon their brows, pulsing as it were with true affection, and they heard his words: "May God bless you and guide you. May God show you favor and be gracious unto you. May God grant you peace." The hands were lifted. "Go with God," he said finally. "And thank you, brothers, for the bread and wine."

As they began to descend the trail his voice came to them faintly on a light evening breeze. "The Lord is my shepherd, I shall not want. He leadeth me . . ."

They spoke very little as they regained the path to Arbel in the gathering dusk. Perhaps it was the lingering effect of their brief visit with the holy hermit. Abram felt filled with grace. He was well pleased to have brought about the encounter and was content to feel upheld in his belief in the Agape's prescience. For his part, Nicolaos had not known what to expect and was somewhat puzzled. The Agape's pronouncements were captivating in the moment; but removed from his presence, they became questionable. He did not doubt the man's sanctity, his sincerity, nor his knowledge of Scripture. But by what authority did one presume to know another man's heart? Confident that he had always practiced humility despite the privilege of his birth, Nicolaos

---

55 Sirach 3:18 NAB

certainly had no ambition or expectation to be "exalted" among men. To the contrary, he was here seeking obscurity and peace. And whatever had the Agape meant by those cryptic words "for now"? Patera was home; nothing could change that.

As night fell they reached a small taberna owned by Christians, with hot food for their bellies and straw pallets for sleeping. By the time he had made his nightly prayers and wearily rested his head where the faint odors of cloves, clean straw and wood smoke would color his dreams, Nicolaos had all but forgotten the enigma of the Agape. In the morning they would make their way to the Arbel Valley and would push on to Capernaum and the Mount of the Beatitudes. He would find solace there; he would dream of that.

XXV

All that he had seen thus far of the Holy Land had not prepared Nicolaos for the grandeur of the Arbel Valley. It was a seat of agriculture, strewn with byways of natural beauty. Here green was not merely a color of the spectrum, but verdant lushness itself; here were trees of every description, fat palms and tall sycamores, oak, fig, almond, pine, tamarisk, carob, fragrant eucalyptus. Here wildflowers beggared the imagination— irises, lilies, pink rockrose, hyacinth; the red, blue and purple anemones were now beginning to fade, but the blue lupin and yellow corn marigolds were rioting forth. They passed many a thriving, well ordered farm on their day's walk, and a prosperous grain mill sporting giant wheels of volcanic basalt, just outside the town.

Capernaum itself was in truth a small city,[56] for it lay alongside the Via Maris, the main trade route between Damascus and Egypt. There was also a strong Roman presence, for it boasted a garrison that housed a detachment of soldiers serving under a centurion. Indeed, the synagogue, the impressive stone structure where Christ had preached, had been built by a Roman centurion.

It followed that this place Nicolaos had pictured as a quiet fishing village was actually a hub of commerce, its streets filled with merchants, travelers, traders, farmers, fishermen, and mercenaries from Phrygia, Gaul and Germany as well as soldiers of Roman blood. Its traffic and lively character reminded him of Patera. Instinctively he made his way to the lakeside at the

---

56 population about 1,500

outskirts of town and discovered an outcropping of stone upon which to sit, overlooking the Sea of Galilee.

"Are you tired, my friend?" Abram asked. He himself was tired; they had been walking all day. Tired and hungry. Taking no immediate answer as an answer, he seated himself next to Nicolaos, and following his lead, removed his sandals and allowed his feet to dangle free in the moist breeze off the water. "We should find shelter, and food."

"I wish to sit for a while, Abram. To observe and to think."

"Aye, it is well. There is much to think about. Saint Peter was born in Bethsaida nearby, but the house he lived in when Jesus called him is here."

Nicolaos nodded. "He called so many apostles here," he said. "Peter and his brother Andrew; John and James, the sons of Zebedee; Matthew."

"Aye."

"It was here that he instructed Peter to pay the temple tax with a coin taken from the mouth of a fish."

"Aye."

"Here that he caused the nets to be filled. Here that he walked upon the waves; this very body of water." It seemed to him the wind upon the lake was murmuring echoed voices; *Duc in altum,* put out into the deep. *Take heart; it is I.*

"It was here that he performed many miracles of healing," Nicolaos said.

"Aye. I recollect the story that he healed Peter's mother-in-law of a fever; and good woman that she was, she immediately rose and began to serve him and others." Abram's stomach growled. "Supper, perhaps."

Nicolaos smiled. "In just a little while, Abram."

They sat in silence several minutes longer while the restive waters lapped the shore in haphazard rhythm. To their left trees downed in a storm combined with drifted sand formed a rough berm to what once was a smooth beach. A purple heron lit upon a jagged upstanding limb to preen itself.

Thoughts of all that had transpired here only a few lifetimes ago, and musings on how much like his favorite childhood space this was, lulled Nicolaos to reverie until encroaching darkness—and the lack here of a light-house—moved him to action.

"Come," he said suddenly, fastening his sandals. "Let us find our rooms."

"Oh, Aye!"

XXVI

The only bath in the village of Nazareth had been a mikvah,[57] available to the community but primarily used for Jewish ceremonial purposes. On their first full day in Capernaum, Nicolaos and Abram availed themselves of one of the Roman public baths. For a blissful hour they soaked in rented bathing attire among other grateful travelers, in relative luxury amidst fluted stone pillars and gaudily painted statues depicting aloof gods and carnal delights.

They explored the market place, busier than that of Patera but small, Abram observed, compared with those in Caesarea. While Abram was choosing an olivewood comb for his wife, Nicolaos noticed a display of little necklaces of small shells strung ingeniously like beads. They stirred a memory of childhood. He purchased two and quietly dropped them into his bag.

At the House of Saint Peter along the Cardo Maximus,[58] now a church and Christian meeting place, Nicolaos was delighted to be asked to speak. Accustomed as he was to addressing multitudes in his uncle's basilica, his deep voice resounded in this smaller space, drawing in passersby, for the church of smooth black basalt was open to the street.

"When first he was called to follow Jesus, Saint Peter did not know that he would be asked to leave this house, to part from his family, to give up his livelihood as a fisherman. He did not understand that he would be called upon to lose his very life so as to serve his God. Peter was no saint in those early days, but a mere man like you and me. Yet somehow he found the courage to do all

---

57 pool of moving water, for ritual cleansing
58 main north-south street of a Roman city, its "heart" (cardo) or economic hub

that; he found it through grace. And in willingly laying down this imperfect existence, he found eternal life."

Abram watched the gathering crowd and exulted in their reaction to this new preacher. Truly Nicolaos possessed a talent from God. Before Abram was married, and again after his second daughter was born, he had visited and worshipped at this church. He had admired the smooth limestone floor and the plastered walls adorned with symbols of both his Jewish heritage and his adopted faith—the shofar and menorah painted alongside the Christian fish and cross—and had tried to decipher the devotional graffiti scratched everywhere in Greek, Latin, Syriac and Aramaic. He knew this church. But never had he witnessed it so alive. The people were upheld by the words they were hearing and by the kindly way in which those words were delivered. It was as though Christ himself or one of the apostles were speaking. Abram felt a thickening in his throat that made it difficult to swallow, and a wetness in his eyes.

Again they tarried, for over the next weeks Nicolaos was asked to speak in the House of Peter several times more. The Christians who made their homes in Capernaum took joy in feting them, each household trying to outdo the last.

Finally with Abram Nicolaos was moved to climb the terraced rise above the city known as the Mount of the Beatitudes. From its height they could survey the Sea of Galilee, glistening as its waters moved beneath the sun, Capernaum nestled like a busy hive along its shore. Mount Hermon to the north and Mount Arbel to the southwest rose gloriously in the distance. Here at the top there was a spreading oak tree where it was good to recline, for in its shade the air was sweet. Nicolaos felt closer here to the Lord than at any other place he had seen, for here Jesus had imparted words of challenge and comfort, words that resonated with him:

You must be perfect, as your heavenly Father is perfect. Love your enemies and pray for those who persecute you. Lay up treasure in heaven, for where your treasure is, there your heart will be also. Everyone who asks, receives. Do not be anxious about your life. Blessed are those who are persecuted for righteousness' sake, for theirs is the kingdom of heaven.

Nicolaos was content to meditate and pray there atop the mount; he could have listened for the Lord's voice all day. Abram respected his companion and remained silent, passing the time with thoughts of his family, remembering the bustle of Caesarea, missing home. The two were quiet and still for so long that a roe deer ventured near, eying them cautiously before returning to a thicket. When a mongoose similarly discovered their presence and was emboldened to come closer to investigate, Abram grew restive and stood. The animal vanished. He stretched and paced for a bit, clearing his throat and sighing.

"You are restless," Nicolaos observed.

Instantly abashed, Abram sat down again. "I do not mean to disturb, your honor."

Nicolaos observed him closely, and in a moment began to smile. "You are missing your family, Abram?"

He felt himself reddening. "I have never been so long away from my wife," he admitted.

Nicolaos rose and stretched himself. "It is well that you miss her; you are blessed."

"Aye," Abram said, flushing the more. "Yet I am privileged to be with you, to guide you."

His companion made the sign of the cross over Abram's head, then rested his hand on his shoulder. "We shall start back in the morning," he said.

XXVII

Miriam was first to see them, from her seat in the dooryard where she was shelling chickpeas: Two weary travelers laden with bags slung over their backs, leaning on their walking staffs. The dark one seemed to notice her, for he straightened and quickened his step.

She called to her daughters, "Come! It's your father! Lord bless him, he is home!"

The children left their play, looked where she pointed, and set out running to greet them, shrieking "Abba!"[59] Miriam entered her kitchen, whisked the morning's leavings from the table, and put a pot of water on the fire to begin a nourishing soup. By the time Abram and Nicolaos crossed the threshold there was wine and cheese to welcome them, and the fragrance of leeks in the pot.

"My husband! Your honor! You have been long expected!" She had pulled herself to attention, tidying her hair and smoothing her garments with unsteady hands; her attempt at decorum lasted but seconds before Abram pulled her into an embrace. "God be praised," she said, her words muffled against his chest.

"I have kept your husband overlong, I suspect," Nicolaos said, "but what a glorious pilgrimage! I am in his debt."

"Aye," Miriam said, surreptitiously wiping her eyes. "I have no doubt of it."

---

59 *father,* in Aramaic

They washed their feet and refreshed their faces while Miriam cut carrots and cabbage for the pot. "Sarah," she said, addressing the elder of the two girls, "Tell our neighbor Apollos to send word to Black Peter," and the child went racing out.

"Black Peter?" asked Abram.

"Aye. Much has happened in your absence. The children have a new friend." Turning toward Nicolaos, "One of your acquaintance, I believe. He has been waiting and watching for your return. He comes to ask about you daily, and I cannot complain of it, for he brings me wood for the fire or beans for the pot, or music to lift my spirits."

"What is this?" Abram looked questioningly at Nicolaos, who was puzzled. "I cannot guess," he said.

She winked at him—quite extraordinary—and said, "Soon you will see."

By the time the vegetables were tender and the bread was brought forth, a lanky dark man in bright green garb and tightly wound turban appeared at the door, aglow with the heat of the day and out of breath. It was the Nubian slave of Cosmas, the stoic. Taking in the scene at the table, he nodded to the men, smiled at the girls, and thrust a small bundle toward Miriam. "Almonds, for the welcoming."

He made a deeper bow before Nicolaos and touched supplicating hands to his forehead. "Peace be upon you, your honor."

"And upon you. But where is your master?"

Peter contorted his face in an effort to temper great joy with a degree of solemnity. "Dead, your honor."

"Dead!"

"The very day we landed in this noble city, before we could make our way to his place of business, he clutched his chest—I hesitate to say 'heart'—and fell to the ground." He demonstrated, thudding his breast and miming a fall, which delighted the girls. "A physician attended him, but by nightfall . . ." Again, joy curbed by restraint.

"Are you a free man, then?"

Unbridled joy now: "Aye! I have the scroll Master Cosmas supplied declaring me free." He patted a fold in his garment. "Also I have the paid passage for my return to Corinth, and my master's paid passage, which may be converted to antoninianii[60] for my use."

"God be praised! I am happy for you."

"Tell him the rest," Miriam prompted.

"Immediately I was free I went to the Christian School in this city." He grinned openly now. "I am baptized. I took the name of Peter. And I wish to serve you."

"To serve me?"

"Aye. My people are Kush, from the Nile Valley, but I was born into slavery in Greece. I have three languages; I served the merchant Cosmas well. And now that I am free and am made Christian, I wish to be of service to you, your honor, the great Nicolaos of Patera!"

Nicolaos could not help but laugh. "I have no need of servants, Peter. But perhaps an assistant with three languages?"

"Ayiee! God is good!" He leapt in the air with all the grace of a dancer. "And there is a vessel leaving with the tide for Myra tomorrow at dawn! If you wish it, I can arrange our passage."

And so it was settled. Peter drew a pan flute from the pleated red band at his waist and began to play a tune, leading the little girls in a merry parade around the room and out the door.

Nicolaos looked at his hosts, bewildered yet relieved to have his immediate needs decided. "It seems I am leaving in the morning."

---

60 Roman coinage

When they retired to their bedchamber Abram presented Miriam with the olivewood comb. In her pleasure as she positioned it to adorn her raven black hair, she was like a bride again. They rested well, once sleep came, and lay abed in the morning as though they had no cares, for their guest had given his blessing and made his farewells the night before, that he might leave without disturbing them at first light.

"Abba! Eema![61] Abba!" Squeals from the children, rushing in to them. "Abba, how good you are!" Sarah exclaimed, fingering a string of pale shells around her neck. Both of the girls had necklaces.

"Not I," said Abram. He looked at his wife, who shook her head. "This is a mystery."

Miriam rose and discovered the bean pot she had scoured clean, set at the foot of their bed. "Abram?" Her eyes were wide with wonder. Astonishingly, inside the pot lay three gold coins.

"Who could have done it?" asked Sarah.

"Black Peter!" said the little one.

Once again there was a lump in his throat and a wetness in his eyes. "I think not," Abram said. "I think not."

---

61 *Mother,* in Aramaic

XXVIII

Bishop Methodius pulled on his beard in frustration. The hour was late, and what remained of his patience was growing thin. Three days he had debated and deliberated with his fellow Lycian bishops from Tyre and Olympos to reach a consensus. The Bishop of Myra was dead, God rest his immortal soul, dead and buried in a crypt beneath this cathedral for two weeks and more, but still no appropriate successor had been agreed upon.

The presbyters of Myra were an incongruous lot; there was no harmony among them. They differed greatly in their talents, if any could truly be termed talented. One had Adoptionistic[62] leanings and another admitted to Diocetism,[63] both unacceptable heresies. A third though married indulged in carnal pursuits. Methodius was strongly devoted to the ideal of virginity in those who represented Christ on earth. Not one of the other men put forth as candidates had the intellect, in his opinion, to succeed the former bishop, and several were simply afraid. Afraid of the responsibility, afraid of the political climate.

"This just won't do, Methodius." His brother bishop from Tyre, ponderous in girth and habitually sardonic in demeanor, was now querulous. "We must reach some agreement."

"Compromise on principles, you mean. No. No, I won't have it." The cathedral space was cavernous when devoid of crowds; his raised voice echoed in the vaulted ceiling.

---

62 Adoptionism was the belief that Jesus was not born the Son of God but was adopted at his baptism, resurrection or ascension
63 belief that Jesus was pure spirit and his physical form an illusion

"Do you propose to rule Myra from your See[64] of Patera? Can you do the work of two men?"

"Of course not. I propose nothing of the sort. But surely we can do better than these who have been nominated. Surely there is someone."

Darkness was overtaking them yet again. The end of the third day! An acolyte moved among them lighting stout candles spaced along the gray stone walls and those on the altar, to push back the shadows.

The Bishop of Olympos was a slight, small man, meek natured. "Perhaps if we prayed upon it again." This was met with silence. "I know you do not wish to hear about my dreams," he continued, "but I was visited again last night."

The Bishop of Tyre groaned.

"It was Jesus. He told me the man we seek will come to us, and his name is Nico."

"Bah! Dreams! And what kind of name is that? It sounds Roman." Methodius grumbled. "That is not a name."

"If he is to come to us," Tyre exclaimed, smirking, "then perhaps we should accept the next priest who walks through the door."

The diminutive Bishop of Olympos smiled sweetly. "Perhaps we should."

"At this hour?" Methodius scoffed.

The acolyte, before retiring from their presence, found his voice: "The fog rises heavily from the sea; it is not a night to be about."

Nevertheless, all three aging prelates turned and watched the entrance.

In what seemed only moments the heavy oaken door was pushed open. A swirl of mist—one could smell the dampness—entered, along with two figures obscured by the shrouding gloom.

"A thousand pardons," the taller figure said. "We saw the light, and wish only to pray."

The three bishops, standing in the shadow of a stone pillar, said nothing.

---

64 local seat of Church jurisdiction

"We are late come from Caesarea Maritima," the other man explained, "and will not tarry long, for we are weary with travel."

Something about that voice! "Come forth," Methodius said. "Step into the light."

The persons who emerged from the darkness were a tall black man gaudily dressed and, in the flowing garb of a Semitic pilgrim—

"Nicolaos!" Methodius also stepped forward.

"Uncle?"

✠

Listening to Uncle Methodius and his fellow bishops with all the patience he could muster, Nicolaos felt increasingly as though he was being swept away on a wave of misguided good intention. Yet his every doubt was met with equally dogged conviction.

"I have no experience with governing even one church, much less an entire diocese."

"But you have a quick mind and a relationship with the Lord," countered Methodius.

"I am young, untried."

"Fresh eyes, new perspectives," said the Bishop of Tyre.

Peter was beaming throughout all this, nodding his head at every encouraging pronouncement from the bishops.

"Have you ever been called Nico?" the Bishop of Olympos asked shyly.

Nicolaos thought for a moment. "I—I think so. Once upon a time, when I was a small child."

Little Olympos clasped his hands together and declared rapturously, "Then it is ordained!"

"My boy," his uncle said, "I have always known you were chosen for great service!"

For a fleeting moment he felt he could not breathe. "For now," the Agape had said. This, if he chose it, would be all he had hoped to avoid. Nicolaos gazed at the cross affixed to the wall behind the altar. "It will come," the Agape had said.

After making a silent, fervent prayer for guidance, he gave his assent.

Thus it was that Nicolaos of Patera, son of Epiphánios and Johanna, beloved former charge of Nonna of Rome, child of God and friend to many, accepted the miter and burden of office as Bishop of Myra. He was 30 years old.

XXIX

Peter of Corinth, or as he delighted in being known, Black Peter, was offered the option of accompanying Bishop Methodius on his return to Patera and serving him there; but he preferred to stay with Nicolaos. "I think you have more need of me," he said.

Because Methodius was not impressed with the men he had met in Myra, "A sorry showing," he promised to send his nephew a presbyter and a deacon from his own See of Patera. "We cannot win hearts and souls if we ourselves are half-hearted."

It was change; it was challenge; it was all a great deal to take in. Nicolaos might have been forgiven had he permitted himself in those early days a retreat into the comfort of reflective solitude. But such was the test, and so perfect was his obedience to God's will that he could not allow himself do so. Instead he set about learning all he could of Myra, the see he had inherited, identifying with the help of God's grace what was good and what needed to be set right. If these efforts made his cross all the heavier, so be it.

What was good in Myra was the enthusiasm of its Christian people. A small core of them responded most favorably to his preaching and eagerly sought his counsel. Here was the strong foundation for his church, he thought. What was bad was an understandable inertia among them, the reluctance to step forward to provide action and leadership. There was an upsurge of anti-Christian sentiment among Romans in Lycia, and even among some native Lycians; the "Little Peace of the Church"[65] was drawing to a close under Diocletian.

Nicholaos felt strongly that the people would respond to beauty and purpose. Within and without, the cathedral church was stark, gray and dismal, an extension of the drab and bleak wharf-side of lower Myra. Myra was the capital of the province of Lycia; Roman rulers and Roman soldiers were everywhere. Little could be done to the exterior of the church without drawing unnecessary attention from the government. But inside! Inside those unadorned walls, much could be accomplished with inspired artistry. He lost no time in sending word to Clodio that carvings were needed, tapestries were desired, sea-glass and shell creations would be welcome.

As for purpose in ministry, it was obvious that this city had suffered during the plague, just as had Patera. There were children orphaned, widows struggling; there was hellish poverty. Clodio could be relied upon to advise on that as well.

And so it transpired that Clodio, who could not plan nor create until he had inspected the need with his own eyes, soon found himself on the road to Myra, sharing transportation—a passenger wagon, drawn by four lumbering mules–with two individuals dispatched by Bishop Methodius.

The first was a presbyter called Alexander, younger even than Nicholaos, newly ordained and pleasant enough, a quiet, serene fellow who seemed perpetually at prayer. The other was the Deaconess Mena, whom Clodio considered prickly and somewhat haughty. He was familiar with her from her frequent visits to the women of their church by the sea, and his wife Vivienne

---

65 four decades of flourishing Christianity beginning with the official edict of tolerance by Gallienus (243-268 A.D.)

liked her. But kind hearted Vivienne liked and approved of everyone. He found the woman difficult to deal with, nearly as difficult as she was to look at.

One could not see for the flowing blue costume she affected in all weathers, but clearly Mena was lame; she walked with a limp, and was supported by a padded crutch beneath her left arm. She was veiled, as befitted her station, but the veil failed to conceal a long face that was coarse and pockmarked and a birthmark, a dark red stain across much of her right cheek. Even her voice was disagreeable, deep and throaty, not light and musical like his wife's. Clodio wondered whether Nicolaos was aware that his uncle was sending him a female deacon, much less such a female.

He had his answer in the look of surprise on his friend's face when the travel weary trio arrived to stand before him.

XXX

Her quarters were adequate, but hardly what she had grown used to in Patera. There was a distinct odor of mildew and a dampness in two of the four walls; only one small barred window that overlooked the harbor. Clearly Bishop Nicolaos had not been informed that she was the one chosen to journey to Myra, to accompany his new presbyter and to assist in the mission of his see. He could not conceal his shock upon greeting her, although he was as welcoming and gracious as ever. There had been few men in her lifetime who had looked on her kindly; certainly no handsome man such as Nicolaos who had looked on her at all for more than a fleeting moment. He was known for his wisdom, though young, and his generosity. She would scrub the mildew and air the room and thank God for the opportunity to serve him.

It had been no small accomplishment to journey thus far on The Way with Christ Jesus. Her mother had died bringing her into the world. Her pagan father would have sold her at birth had she been unmarked and whole. It was his belief that she was cursed by Vulcan, ugliest of the Roman gods, who was himself lame. Had a Christian serving woman in the household not taken pity upon her, fed her and bound her poor twisted foot that she might one day learn to walk after a fashion, she surely would not have lived past infancy. And had that woman not ultimately taken Mena into her own home, she would not have survived to make her own way.

She owed an immeasurable debt to her foster mother and the community of believers who had made a place for her in their lives and found useful work for her in their world. Even more importantly, they had allowed her

113

to learn, and so to grow in graces. She had heard first of the life of Job, who suffered much and railed at God yet persevered, and through her own trials she came to draw solace from that story. But when she learned of the pure love of Jesus, her heart was claimed and her future was made. The longer she devoted herself to Him, the lesser her trials seemed to be. The headaches came less frequently now, and she no longer trembled in the company of those who found her too different to be worthy of notice.

She would minister to the women here, and act as chaperone for presbyters among women; and if there were other duties she could perform to the glory of God, she would fulfill them joyfully. As for men—and women and children, for that matter—who were shortsighted enough to judge her on appearances, she would tolerate them or win them over. But she would not suffer fools. Nor would she bend, nor ever break.

XXXI

"Even the morning light does little to brighten this place," Clodio observed. "You are right. Your church needs something beautiful for God."

"Do you think your colleagues can help?" Nicolaos was hopeful.

"I know they can. There are artisans in Patera who can work wonders with cloth and color. For the church—for you—they will donate their labors, or give a very good price."

They were standing in a broad shaft of light from a high window, a weak and watery stream of illumination that lacked the potency of the sun. "Behind the crucifix," Clodio said, "a wooden backdrop—I have just the piece of red oak—and candle stands of carved oak on the wall to either side, all of the wood burnished and set with polished tin to reflect the light."

"Yes! And tapestry banners in the blues and greens of the seas, our Mediterranean and the Sea of Galilee."

"It will be a gift to heaven, Sea Turtle—pardon me, Bishop Sea Turtle," Clodio said to his grinning friend. "When we are finished the Lord will hold it to his heart and smile."

Nicolaos felt truly encouraged for the first time in the months since accepting the bishopric. It was good to have friends. "There is another matter," he said. "Come!" He strode to the entrance, with Clodio following, and threw open the heavy wooden doors. "There!" he said, pointing in the direction of a marble edifice. "Do you see that white building?"

"A pagan temple!"

"Aye. A temple to Artemis, Greek goddess of the hunt, among other claims." He turned to Clodio with a look of triumph. "I led Peter and some of the men of the congregation in pulling down her statue and destroying other stone ornaments within."

Clodio's eyes widened in disbelief. "Will you not be punished?"

"Devotion to Artemis in these parts has fallen away to nothing. The temple had become a gathering place for vandals and thieves. Had it been dedicated to the Roman goddess of the hunt Diana, there might have been retribution; but as it is, Rome has looked away."

"And to what end did you do this, Nicolaos? Such things are an offense to the Lord, but in Lycia they are everywhere."

"For the building, Clodio. That building will make an excellent refuge for orphans and widows, a home such as you and Vivienne have provided in Patera."

Clodio began to see the logic here. "And who will preside over them?"

"Alexander, the new presbyter, is eager. The Deaconess Mena will recruit women to help him. I am sure that in time it will be a success. You are still pleased with your mission, are you not?"

"Oh, aye. It has grown and is thriving."

"As your own family is thriving?"

Clodio could not resist beaming with pride. "Vivienne is again with child, and little Nicolaos is walking. You should see how he walks, like a prowling leopard!" This made him think of Mena. "You are content with your uncle's assignment of the deaconess?"

Nicolaos nodded. "She is willing and able. I have seen her work with the women of Patera. She will be an asset here."

"So then, you are not put off?"

"I do not know what you mean."

"Her lameness, Sea Turtle, is one thing. But her manner is rough, and her face—"

Nicolaos dropped a hand on his friend's shoulder. "I see the face of one who is close to God," he said.

Humbled, Clodio lowered his eyes and hung his head. "Forgive a reckless Scorpion, whose sting is ever at the ready," he said. "I had forgotten." He looked up into his friend's steady and kindly gaze. "Forgotten how good you are, holy Bishop."

XXXII

Clodio was as reliable as his word. Within the year he and his artisan friends in Patera had provided all the beauty Nicolaos had envisioned for his cathedral in the harbor district of Myra. There were tapestry banners that depicted the life of Christ and many of his parables. The altar area was embellished with polished wood carvings and wondrous reflected light. Bits of sea glass and translucent shells had been installed in the corners of the high windows to create beams of color without obstructing the view of God's sky. Black Peter often harmonized with their worship song on his pan pipes, and in time he was joined by a player on the cithara.[66] The grateful congregation grew steadily, in active membership and in sincere devotion; many from outside their community were instructed and baptized.

Alexander too had proved worthy of the trust placed in him, as had the Deaconess Mena, who was no stranger to hard work. The former temple of Artemis was transformed into a welcoming refuge for unfortunates and a place where adults as well as children might learn of The Way. Mena was successful in pressing other women of the assembly into service and in training older children in the care of little ones, so that the greatest number of children might be housed and helped. Lycian families in the surrounding neighborhood were pleased to see an end to criminal activity at the old temple site and did not hesitate to do their part by sharing food and clothing. Black Peter was of invaluable assistance to the mission, for the children loved him. There seemed to be nothing that could not be accomplished with the help of fellow believers and the Lord. Nicolaos felt truly blessed.

---

66 most popular and versatile stringed instrument of the day

The four of them—the bishop, the new presbyter, the deaconess, and the man of all trades, Black Peter—made their home in the bishop's residence behind the church, an arrangement that seemed natural and productive. They often took their meals together, particularly in the evenings, when the day's work was discussed.

✠

"A centurion crossed our threshold today," Alexander said. They were sharing cena[67] before twilight prayers. "The children were at their lessons—in Latin, thankfully. He asked a few questions and went away. Pleased, I think."

"Or at least, not displeased," Mena said.

"It is to be expected," Nicolaos assured them. "We are always under the watchful eye of Rome. So long as we are peaceable and there are no incidents to draw attention, we are relatively safe."

Peter helped himself from a dish of cucumbers, cabbage and leaks in vinegar. "Incidents may be unavoidable if we do not fashion doors that may be bolted after dark," he said. "The wharf district still is unsafe for decent women. Only yesterday two drunken men, seamen by the look of them, stumbled in and accosted the deaconess with their foul talk."

Mena bowed her head and murmured, "It was nothing." In truth, the men had left in disappointment, laughing and muttering vague obscenities, when once they had seen her face.

"Why am I hearing of this only now?"

"It was of no moment, bishop," she said.

"I disagree. Alex, take care of the matter of doors in the morning. There is lumber to be had near the dockside, and what cannot be appropriated to

67 supper

120

our purposes may be purchased. Arsenios has sent me another sum for our collective purse. Small, but adequate to our needs."

"Aye, Bishop Nicolaos."

"And make sure there are stout locks, with keys enough for the four of us; there is an ironmonger among our congregation."

"I shall see to it."

Mena bristled at this exchange. She did not wish to be viewed as weak, nor did she welcome the attentions of "protectors." "No moment," she muttered again, under her breath.

Not for the first time Nicolaos harkened back to Clodio's warning description of the deaconess, as rough in demeanor. He had grown used to her silences, her gruffness when addressed; the way her jaw set with stubbornness when opposed. "It is decided, deaconess."

Her dark eyes met his for a moment, defiant yet sad. She dropped her gaze quickly, and her response was all meekness. "Yes, Bishop."

He saw that she was still defensive, however, for her hands clenched and her lips were pressed in a hard line. "We have to consider those who help you as well," he said kindly. "And the children."

She looked at him again, strangely, he thought.

Of course, she was thinking. Those who are truly valued. Those who would not have been dismissed by drunken men with disgust. Or with laughter.

"What is it?" Nicolaos asked.

"Nothing, Bishop." She unclenched her fists and put her hands in her lap, where they could not be seen. "You are right. We must have safety."

She would not meet his gaze again but remained quiet throughout the rest of the meal. It should be more pleasant to have a woman here among us, Nicolaos thought fleetingly. There should be a nurturing softness, a presence like unto a blend of the sisters of Bethany, Mary and Martha. Surely the fault lay with himself. He would pray about it.

XXXIII

There came a day when Deaconess Mena was grateful for stout doors with locks, and for the attentions of "protectors." The rowdy seamen who had accosted her did not return, nor did any Roman soldier; but there was one man who seemed to be increasingly obsessed with the mission, and who began to make his obsession known. He was a familiar face in the community, a native Lycian butcher who supplied the Roman garrison, manager if not also owner of a slaughterhouse and market near the wharf.

It all began with the man behaving strangely, loitering near the former temple in the early morning, watching and murmuring curses upon Christians. On the second such day he shouted obscenities at the women who entered the mission to assist there, while chanting loud appeals to the god Artemis for aid in his "hunting." He was a mountain of a man, towering and muscular, but ordinarily peaceable and thus unremarkable. Now he was become a menacing, wild-eyed hulk, loud and disheveled, his cloak and toga stained with blood. Passersby gave him a wide berth; he seemed to be quite mad. Always he appeared when the men were away. For fear of burdening them unnecessarily, Mena did not mention these scenes at home. Words were not deeds. She prayed for the man, for he was surely possessed.

But on the third day, while Alexander was in the heart of the city visiting the sick, when the deaconess and two helpers were escorting children back from morning devotions at the church, the butcher was suddenly at the mission entrance. Mena hastily unlocked the door and was about to follow the others she had ushered inside when she was shoved. Her crutch flung askew, she lost her footing and tumbled to the ground, striking her head on a cobblestone. Dazed from that blow, she was aware that the man had stepped over her. With the cries of the women and children buzzing in her ears, she raised her head and beheld the butcher lumbering toward the wharf with three small wriggling boys in his arms.

The cathedral doors burst open. Mena rushed in, distraught and out of breath, leaning heavily upon her crutch; a swelling bruise was already ripening on her temple.

"Come quickly, please! The children!"

Nicolaos had been at prayer, Peter polishing a candlestick. "What is wrong, Deaconess?" the bishop asked.

"A man, the butcher from the wharf road, has stolen three of our smallest boys!"

"For slaves?" Peter asked.

"For much worse, I am afraid. He is mad, possessed by a demon, surely."

"The wharf road, you say?" Nicolaos was on his feet, gesturing to Peter.

"I know the place," Peter said.

"As do I. Go!"

Peter pelted out the doors and down the cobbled street, his long strides quickly outdistancing the bishop. The sight of the brightly garbed, tall black man from the cathedral racing, then the robed bishop running, and finally the veiled holy woman hobbling along behind them caused a commotion and drew a following. Exclamations of "orphans stolen!" "Christian mission!" and "the mad butcher who serves the Romans!" caused several men and even a few women to run in the direction of the wharf.

By the time Nicolaos reached the slaughterhouse, the mob had closed on the butcher and was chasing him toward the quay. Nicolaos entered the building and immediately was struck by the dank, oppressive odor of mud, blood, singed hair, damp wool, and decay. Skinned carcasses of pigs and sheep were hanging from the rafters, and in the dim light he beheld an empty cauldron over cold coals and a barrel filled with brine. In the barrel three small bruised heads were almost submerged. With all his strength he tipped the barrel to drain it and then lifted the little bodies to the ground.

"Evil, be gone! Holy God, restore these lives, please heal these innocents! In the name of Jesus, live and be well!"

The children coughed and sputtered and opened reddened eyes just as Mena entered. She pulled the long scarf from her head and tenderly covered their nakedness.

"Clean water!" she commanded, never taking her gaze from their frightened faces.

Nicolaos found a wooden pail, splashed the water in it from his palm to his mouth to be sure it was pure, and brought it to her. She poured it over the boys' eyes and ears and dried their faces with her garments.

Black Peter appeared then, with a crowd gathering behind him.

"The butcher?" Nicolaos asked.

"Dead." Peter was shaken. "A rock was thrown. He fell to the stones beneath the pilings."

Nicolaos felt hot tears coming. A soul, once innocent as these three, lost to sin.

He hung behind after Peter and the others had carried the children away and the women among them had helped Mena leave, supporting her on either side. He went to the wharf and descended to the rocks below, but the butcher's body had been taken away. So much revolting sin, so much evil in the world, so much beyond comprehension that was sickening! Leaning against the barnacled pilings with the stench of the barrel's brine on his robes, he felt his gorge rising and found himself retching into the dark waters of the surf. He remembered the other time he had raced through city streets, only to arrive too late and find his parents already dead. He reflected that he would have tried to cast out the demon, had he reached that poor sinner first. And he thought of how amazingly strong Mena had been, yet gentle with the children; how, when she ripped off her veil her light brown hair had fallen long, wavy and shining; and how, with her face lit with concern beyond her own cares, she was . . . beautiful.

XXXIV

The events of that day were reported, distorted, repeated and enhanced throughout the province of Lycia and beyond. In time it was asserted that the boys had been raised from the dead; that their bodies had been cut into pieces before being brined, yet were raised whole. There eventually would evolve the tale that they had been dismembered and dead for seven years when discovered by Nicolaos of Myra and restored to life. Such is the hunger of men for mystery!

Had the children indeed been dead when he prayed over them? He did not know. He knew only that they survived their ordeal and lived to grow taller and stronger in faith. He knew that he and they had been blessed by the Holy Spirit in that moment. He knew that a woman's loveliness had little to do with physical appearance.

And one other thing he knew: It was disconcerting and disheartening that, due to his relative youth, in his notoriety he was becoming known, even by Rome, as "the Boy Bishop."

He began to grow a beard.

Mena held misgivings and doubts deep in her heart. She felt she had failed the children in her charge. It occurred to her that her disability had put them in danger. Had she been able to move more quickly, perhaps she could have kept the boys from being taken. She wondered too whether her intemperate attitude and low spirits affected her service. It was not that she minded menial work, only that there was so much of it; with every day her strength was sapped and her leg ached unbearably. Hauling water, scrubbing floors, tending children and women fairer than she, women who had known the love of men, invited thoughts of jealousy. She was constantly reminding herself that Jesus said, whatever you do for the least of these you do for Me. She was forever failing in charity, and asking pardon.

And she began to question her instincts about others. Clearly she had misjudged the bishop in thinking even for a moment that she was not valued. Indeed, she should not have been so impudent as to judge him at all. He had always treated her fairly and kindly. Of late his interest seemed warmer, and as much as she rejoiced in that, it somehow made her afraid.

"Perhaps I should seek different lodgings," she offered suddenly one early morning. "Perhaps rooms shared with other women would be more appropriate. Or I could stay at the mission."

They had broken their fast before the sun breached the horizon. Nicolaos was still muddle headed from sleep and did not immediately respond.

"Have I made myself a nuisance, Deaconess?" Peter asked earnestly. "I know my bleating on the pipes is not to everyone's taste."

"Of course not. I treasure your music."

"Is it I?" Alexander asked. "Have I been rude, sister, or crude in my manner? I was raised among men, with my father and only brothers at home. My brashness is not purposeful."

Mena shook her head. "No, no, there is no fault in anyone here. I—I simply think—it has occurred to me that appearances—" She looked to her bishop for a saving word and hearing none, continued to stammer like a bashful young girl. "I—I miss the company of other women."

Nicolaos, jarred fully awake now, was studying her closely. Her head was healed from her fall on the street, but her face was flushed, making the birthmark darker. Her lovely hair was hidden beneath her veil, as was customary. "You work with women at the mission," he said. "Throughout the community you are with women. Women are the reason you are here."

"Yes." Her embarrassment was increasing; she cast a pleading glance in his direction.

He felt a sudden tenderness toward her, seeing her thus discomfited, she who was normally so self-assured. And as that feeling of tenderness welled, he thought he understood.

"Make other arrangements if you wish it, Mena," he said softly. "But we shall miss you."

It was the first occasion in all this time that she had heard him speak her name, and the sweetness of it only strengthened her resolve. She would move into the mission.

And the truth of the statement offered in charity struck Nicolaos with a vague sadness. He would indeed miss her. What would his friend the Scorpion make of that?

XXXV

"Precautions should be taken," Clodio said. They were seated comfortably in the courtyard of the great yellow stone house above the Patera lighthouse cliff that was only now, after nearly two years in residence, beginning to feel like home. He was entertaining Arsenios, the friend who oversaw the family shipping concern that had come to Bishop Nicolaos through his father. "It is only wise for business, and prudent for our families. We must consider drastic measures." He glanced at little Nicolaos and Irene playing quietly in the shade. "A man's outlook in life changes once he has children."

Arsenios nodded. He had come here for advice because Clodio was native to Lycia and was known to have a vast understanding of the land and its history. It was common knowledge that the Imperator Diocletian had ordered Manicheans in Egypt burned alive along with their scriptures. Christians were now forbidden from the bureaucracy as well as the military, in order to appease the Roman gods. The news had circulated that upon his arrival in Antioch in the autumn,[68] Diocletian had ordered that the Deacon Romanus lose his tongue for failing to denounce his Lord Jesus Christ. The Imperator had since returned to his palace in Nicodemia to spend the winter, accompanied by Emperor Galarius, who fostered a great hatred for Christians and wished to exterminate them from the earth. Romanus, whose mouth would not heal, was said to be resigned to eventual execution. It was generally understood that a universal persecution was coming.

---

68 302 A.D.

"There are rumors," Arsenios ventured, "that there is life to be lived in safety underground."

"Not rumors," Clodio countered. "It is fact. I have gone beyond the caves and seen it for myself. Whole communities, not hiding but thriving."

Arsenios's pulse quickened and he felt hopeful for the first time in a very long while. "To the east?"

"There is Matiate, the "city of caves,"[69] to the east, yes, but there are others; one near unto Patera."

"And we will be allowed there?"

Clodio beamed with confidence. "My friend, not merely allowed but welcomed." He called to Vivienne to join them and to bring the wine flask and their deepest cups. They were about to form an alliance.

In Myra the signs of the times were no less cautionary, but there would be no refuge for the bishop or his presbyters. Nicolaos knew that a time of great trial was coming, but his place was among the people, for his vocation was one of service.

Rather than decreasing his public acts or concealing his objectives, he had recently dismantled two more pagan temples within the city, freeing them for use as orphanages and places of refuge for the poor, Christian and non-Christian alike.

The Deaconess Mena had taken up residence in their first mission near the cathedral, which was a blessing to the children there. Much of her day was spent training and counseling others who would supervise operations at the newer locations. She still frequently took her meals at the bishop's residence,

---

69 largest of over 40 subterranean cities in Türkiye, where 60-70,000 people lived in hiding

however, much to the delight of Nicolaos, Peter and Alexander, for when she ate with them she usually also cooked. She had mastered the art of baking the gastrin his mother Johanna's kitchen had been known for, which brought Nicolaos great pleasure.

They were enjoying those pastries after a particularly filling evening meal when Nicolaos felt called to broach an uncomfortable subject. The four were seated on chairs Roman fashion about a table bathed in light from a suspended chandelier of many candles. Black Peter's garb of vibrant reds and greens was especially lustrous in their glow. Young Alexander's face in partial shadow took on an air of maturity, and Mena's countenance was softened, made strangely fetching by candlelight.

"We must speak of necessity about the unrest that is coming," he began. "We all know what a persecution can mean. There is no reason to believe that the next will be any less severe than the last."

Alexander moved into full light; his face was suddenly drained of all color. Mena's back stiffened and she pressed her lips into a defiant line. Only Peter looked uncertain, confused.

"I have no doubt that all of you will meet any test. You will not deny Christ to save yourselves—"

They murmured as of one voice. "No. No. Certainly not."

"But our God knows there are limits to human endurance; remember that in his mercy he forgives all."

"I will never deny my Lord Jesus!" exclaimed Peter.

"And we would not ask that of you, Peter." He smiled at his earnest friend. "But this I will ask of you: If I am taken—and it is likely that I will be—I want you to use your cunning to escape. You need only speak in the tongue of your fathers—"

"Kush," said Peter.

"—to confound the Romans. Keep your eyes open but close your ears to our enemies, and stay your tongue. Speak no word of Greek or Latin or any other commonly recognized language, and behave as though you do not understand what is happening. In that way you may get away and live long to serve your Lord. Your faith is your strength, but your—forgive me—your strangeness is your best defense."

Peter considered, and nodded.

"You, Mena, must take the children and hide yourselves among the households of the congregation. Forego your veil—"

"I will not!"

He raised a hand to silence her. "Forego your veil and other trappings of The Way. I have heard from Arsenios and Clodio, whom you remember, and they may have a plan for you, and for as many presbyters as may be in danger."

"And you?" Mena asked. Her eyes were glistening.

"I will follow where Jesus leads me," he said.

XXXVI

And Jesus led him to the people, to the streets. Fearing nothing more than the thought of lost opportunity, he made himself seen, sometimes accompanied by Black Peter, sometimes quite alone. He walked to the far reaches of Myra and beyond, into the districts shunned by most members of his congregation, engaging all manner of people, helping where he could, spreading God's word with kindness. In a relatively short time he gained fame throughout the city and lower Lycia as a peacemaker, a wise friend, a generous man.

Is there a dispute among you? The Christian Bishop Nicolaos is sure to find a solution fair to all. Are you in desperate straits, in search of honest work? Bishop Nicolaos may have the answer. Have you not eaten, slept, felt well for some time? There are places Bishop Nicolaos has opened to the least of us, with help and sustenance and no demand for repayment. Perhaps all you need is prayer, although you did not realize that was what you needed until you met him, Nicolaos. Bishop Nicolaos of Myra!

"Your fame precedes you, holy man." This from a Roman soldier, a bugler by the look of his uniform and accouterments, towering over him not in malice but with curiosity. "How is it you do not skulk in the shadows, practicing your foreign superstition, as do most like you?"

Nicolaos considered carefully before speaking. "The Way of Christ is no superstition," he said, "but a formula for life well lived in truth."

"I had a friend in my century[70] who practiced it," the man admitted, somewhat reluctantly, "before Christians were excised from the ranks."

---

70 a military unit of 100 soldiers

Nicolaos nodded. "We are friends to all."

The soldier seemed to be assessing him, frowning, then motioned his desire to withdraw from the street and its midday crowd. Nicolaos followed him to a quiet alley between two market stalls.

"There is a woman," he began, "kindred to the friend I mentioned, reputed to be also a believer. She carries a child that is—is not wanted, that she must be rid of." His voice lowered. "I can pay."

"The apostles have taught that we shall not kill a child by obtaining an abortion, nor destroy him after he is born. It is—"[71]

The soldier held up a staying hand. "I do not wish to hear your views," he said abruptly. "I simply want to know, will you help me?"

"No." Nicolaos looked long and hard into the soldier's eyes, until the man dropped his own. "I will not help you to do murder. But I will help the woman. Do you know the mission in the old temple across from my church near the harbor?"

"I have seen it."

"Have her come there. She will be seen to and you will not be troubled with her care."

"And the child?"

"Also seen to. And you will not be troubled."

This seemed to satisfy, for the soldier executed a cursory salute, turned on his heel, and disappeared back into the crowds.

---

71 The Didache (The Teaching of the Twelve Apostles, c. 80-140 A.D.)

And so it happened that Deaconess Mena found herself in charge of yet another young woman, not a helper nor a pupil but one in need of aid. The woman's name was Zelle; a Lycian, no longer a maiden child but not yet old, and comely when she smiled, which was seldom. She was a passive little thing, no stranger to The Way but hardly devoted to it. Neither bold nor submissive, indifferent to the babe in her womb and to others about her, she seemed aloof and only marginally grateful for a safe place to sleep while she was large with child and for decent food to eat. When Zelle lapsed into fever and died giving birth, Mena baptized the babe, calling him Joseph. It comforted the deaconess to believe that through the baptism of the child, the mother's sins were also forgiven.[72]

Although another among the helpers was enlisted as wet nurse, the deaconess cared for the child in every other respect. She softened as her heart filled with love and wonder at the Lord's mysterious ways. She began to think of herself as Joseph's true mother. And while she chastised herself for indulging in flights of fantasy, it nevertheless pleased her immensely to think secretly of Bishop Nicolaos, who had brought Zelle to her, as Joseph's surrogate father. She lavished all the affection of which she had always felt deprived in her own life on the child.

And thus having gained a "family" of her own, Mena began to accept the notion of an escape plan.

---

72 in accordance with the letters of Cyprian of Carthage, 253 A.D.

She began to think of herself as Joseph's true mother.

XXXVII

"This is amazing!" Clodio exclaimed. "Truly, truly beyond all imagining."

His escort beamed with pride. "It is staggering when you first behold it," he said. "I felt the same myself."

They were deep inside the earth in a cool room of hewn limestone as large as that in which he and Vivienne slept at the yellow house. Below the earth, yet not in darkness nor suffocating closeness, for there were lamps affixed everywhere and ventilation shafts that circulated air from the ground level.

"Most of the rooms are natural caves," his guide said, "but some, like this one, are manmade, as are the tunnels and passages connecting them."

Clodio was admiring a wall mural depicting a garden. Muted tones of green foliage and blue skies, brightened with vividly colorful flowers of every season rioting together.

"We have much artwork here, Clodio, particularly in the sanctuaries and worship spaces. You will not see finer in any church in Patera."

"And there are other levels?"

"There are many. We have stables, grain silos, a market, even tombs. There are three centralized wells for water and two pools for bathing. Five entrances other than the one by which you came, all well concealed. Our people have hidden from invaders for hundreds of years, Clodio, in underground cities like this. This is how Lycians have survived."

"And now Christians."

His new friend nodded solemnly. "Now Christians, and Jews, and Manicheans. The reach of Rome is vast, but so far the legions have not discovered the rebellion beneath their feet."

Clodio looked about him again. It was possible. It was almost inviting. "My wife Vivienne and I have two children, but there are many more in our household, and we have trusted friends. There are chambers enough?"

The man clapped a reassuring hand on his shoulder. "You shall have what you need."

At his workspace in the old office of Epiphánios above the Patara harbor Arsenios took parchment, pen and ink in hand and began to write:

Holy Bishop Nicolaos, I will this day safeguard as much of your fortune as I may, for future good works and for the Church. I leave the running of your esteemed father's business to a man who is neither pagan nor Christian but is a good, honest soul and no friend of Rome. He has served us well for many years and may be trusted. More I cannot tell you, for many innocent lives may soon be in jeopardy and could be lost if secrets are not kept. But know that those who love you appeal to our Savior daily for your own safety and will continue to do so until we meet again.

Your servant and friend since the days of your childhood,

Arsenios

XXXVIII

The scrap of parchment from Clodio was even more cryptic:

The scorpion burrows early this year. Pray God it will not be a long winter. My Vivienne is again with child! Am I not the most blessed among men? Peace be with you, my holy friend.

Nicholaos took both messages to the brazier in the kitchen and watched them wither and die away on the coals. He did not want to know more; indeed, it would be foolhardy even to speculate. He lifted the souls of his friends in prayer and asked his Lord Jesus to strengthen their resolve and see to their safety.

Looking about, he helped himself to a bit of stale bread and found honey for dipping. It had been weeks, perhaps months, since the deaconess had favored them with her presence and her cooking skills. He missed her baking nearly as much as he missed her acerbic yet compliant nature and the provocative thoughts she never hesitated to share.

He had asked Alexander about her absence only a few evenings before.

"She now spends most of her time and energies caring for the babe Joseph."

"Zelle's child?"

Alex shook his head. "Mena's boy, decidedly. It is as though she has adopted him. It is wondrous to see. Our sister has been softened by motherliness, I think."

Black Peter agreed. "It is a miracle. She has not been short with me since the baby came."

Nicolaos had pondered this development and worded his comments carefully: "Please communicate to her that she is still welcome at our table, and that she may bring the babe."

"Babies cry," said Peter.

"Nevertheless."

The bread was very dry, and the honey did little for it.

XXXIX

Mena did not venture back to that masculine fold until Joseph was sitting up unassisted and could amuse himself with a toy braided from brightly colored rags. He was a sturdy, robust child, cheerfully quiet by nature, and no trouble to her. No trouble at all. If on occasion he attempted to pull himself up by her skirts, she merely distracted him with beads to clack or a pomegranate to roll. She thought wistfully that she might teach him one day to knead dough, or to shell peas or pound grain, just as she would teach him to pray. Perhaps knowing of his lineage, one of the helpers at the mission had thoughtlessly observed, "What a strong child! What a fine little soldier he will make," and Mena had barely conquered the impulse to fly at her in a rage.

The bishop appreciated the child's unique qualities, she was sure of it. Joseph learned so quickly and was so fair to look upon, one had to take notice. Bishop Nicolaos had given him a large smooth cowrie shell to play with and did not begrudge her the time she devoted to his care. In fact, he had paid her what she considered the ultimate compliment.

It was at the first cena they all shared together at the residence since the child's birth. Joseph was seated contentedly in her lap. "It is well that you are among us again," the bishop had said. Alex and Peter readily agreed, nodding and managing to mumble "Aye" while their mouths were stuffed with fresh bread.

"And it is well that you keep this little one near you," he had continued. The bishop's eyes had been soft and warm. He lay a hand for a moment upon the child's head; and while he maintained silence, she knew he was praying a blessing upon him. "I think that God holds dear those gentle souls who show loving kindness to the innocent among us," he said.

She had been overwhelmed with affection for both the man and the child, and held fast to that memory.

The persecution was drawing nearer. Word came that in February[73] the newly built church in Nicodemia had been razed, its Scriptures torched, its treasures seized. A new edict forbade Christians from assembling for worship throughout the entire empire. Christian Imperial freedmen were being re-enslaved, and no one who professed the Christ any longer held citizen rights, by order of the Imperator Diocletian. By spring and Resurrection Day those who would not renounce the Lord and sacrifice to the gods of Rome were being burned alive in Palestine. Nearer to home, rebellions were put down in Melitene.[74]

With the urging of Bishop Nicolaos, Mena made contact with a family that had an evacuation plan. She knew no details of the scheme but understood that theirs was the escape route approved by the friends of the bishop as the best chance for herself and for Joseph. And yet, reluctant to leave her duties, she remained at the mission, and worshipped in secret, and served her friends at the residence as best and as often as she could, seeking normalcy in routine.

And then, in the summer a second edict was published, ordering the imprisonment of all bishops and priests.

---

73 303 A.D.
74 an Anatolian city east of Myra; Malatya, Türkiye

XL

The reckoning, when it came, was swift as the whirlwind before the rising gale that blows off the southern sea. One moment he was in meditation with his Lord before the altar, and the next he was in chains. Only the day before he had been tolerated, by some in Myra even revered; and now he was disgraced, demeaned, and dragged from his church, a criminal. The legionaries who seized him, helmeted and armed, never more fearsome, handled him roughly; and even as they did so, he forgave them. They had been taught in ignorance, after all, that Christians such as he were plotting enemies of Rome, cannibals who ate flesh and drank blood in their rituals, an abomination to right thinking men. He looked about for Alexander as he stumbled into the street and saw him similarly bound, struggling with his captors. "Do not resist," he called out, certain that resistance would be met with further violence. In the tumult he could not be sure that Alex heard him.

As he was pushed and pulled away from the wharf district Nicolaos saw the mission deserted, its once substantial wooden door broken and hanging at a drunken angle off its hinges. Inside could be glimpsed beds upset, clothing and clay jars strewn about in disarray. The children were nowhere to be seen, nor the helpers, nor Peter. And not Mena.

She could not keep up. In her anguish she realized that grave truth, and with it the sobering knowledge that, should she lose sight of those she was following, all would be lost. Mena cried out loudly, and the lone woman among the guides slowed her pace. There was terror in the woman's face, yet she stopped. "Take him," Mena said, thrusting forth the bundle that was Joseph.

There was commotion behind them, sounds of pursuit becoming louder. With pity now overcoming fear and with sorrow in her eyes, the woman did as bidden. "God be with you, sister," she said as she turned and raced for the forest beyond the city.

Mena began to walk diagonally away from the direction the others had taken. Her foot and leg throbbed badly, and the crutch with which she hobbled had rubbed a soreness beneath her arm. Much as she wished to remain veiled, she pulled down her head covering, loosing her hair, her one beauty. From the folds of her robe she withdrew a copper comb studded with bits of colored glass and placed it at her temple, in hopes of transforming her appearance. Hastily she grabbed at a clump of poppies and nearly spent windflowers, clutching them close to her breast as she walked on.

"Halt!" Two Roman soldiers had come up quickly behind her. "What are you about, woman?"

She answered in Latin, "Only walking in the twilight, gathering flowers."

The larger of them noted her crutch. "With that, you walk for pleasure?"

"Not for pleasure but for healing; the act is medicine to me."

"Healing?" Drawing his sword, he used it to raise her skirts, exposing her bound clubfoot.

"Wouldst thou make sport of me?" She asked, faintly smiling. The longer she could detain these two, the better for her friends.

The other soldier examined her closely. "I know this one. She was with the bishop the day he performed his sorcery at the slaughterhouse."

Mena hung her head.

"Are you sure?"

The other snorted. "Who could forget that face?"

Silently, she prayed, *My Jesus, deliver Joseph to safety.*

The soldier who had drawn his weapon now holstered it and fumbled for a small object which he held under her nose. "Observe. An amulet of Jupiter. Make obeisance to it."

Mena did nothing.

"Kiss it!" he commanded.

Slowly she raised her head. "I will not," she said.

"Christian dog!" the second man exclaimed.

A crushing blow to the back of her head, a blinding light behind her eyes.

Her last thoughts were of the boy.

XLI

Wherever Vivienne looked, all was stone, all was gloom. Above, below, beside her, gray hewn rock. No sky, no sand or earth, no growing things. She had foolishly brought with her a jasmine vine preserved from her mother's garden, in hopes that the potted treasure might thrive under lantern light, much as it had in sunlight at the yellow house. Within a fortnight it was dead, and she had wept as though she had lost a friend.

She felt an overwhelming sadness, a loss she feared would surely mark her baby, but in moments of solitude she could not stay her tears. Tears that fell on the woolen yarns she worked to bring a bit of softness, a touch of color, to their living space. It was all she could do, and it would not be enough.

And there was the chill that crept into their bones. She stitched cloaks and heavy coverlets to drive away the pervasive cold, but naught could warm her broken heart.

Little Nicolaos was happy, for he had found other children to play with him; and Irene was content, with her toys about her and her mother's close attention. But the babe yet to be born? How could he not feel his mother's melancholy in the womb? And what kind of life would this child be able to live without knowing the world above?

They had heard that Bishop Nicolaos was taken prisoner, and all his good works lost, his church smashed and burned. She tried to keep her despair from her husband, but when that news reached them it was as though a dam had broken. She had sobbed in Clodio's arms.

"Why, Clodio? Why? Why did not the Lord protect him, of all men?"

"Perhaps he did," Clodio had said. "Perhaps he will."

"It is hard to keep faith with 'perhaps.'" She had felt she would strangle with the weight of it if she did not say it: "And what of us? What will become of us? Where is God in all of this? How can he allow those who love and serve him to be struck down, or burrow for their lives like worms? Oh, Clodio! To let our child be born in a cave, among strangers!"

"As his own Son was?"

He had lifted her chin and kissed her tenderly. Her husband too was near weeping, but his belief and his determination were strong. He had covered her face with kisses until her mood lifted. For a time.

Clodio was right, of course. But so was she.

Peter had curled himself into a ball and pressed his body deep under a rock ledge, so that he might sleep in relative safety and peace. When he had heard the news that the cathedral and mission had been raided by Roman soldiers and the bishop taken away, he had removed from the city with only the clothes on his back and the few coins he carried with which to buy rations. He felt a fear like none before in his life. Until he was freed by the death of his master his most basic needs had always been met, for he had been a valuable chattel; and since coming under the protection of the Christians he had been part of a family. But it appeared that his family was to be no more. He traveled far that first day, and still farther the second, and the third.

He had turned his garments so that the bright colors were on the inside, next his body, in order to be less noticeable. Remembering what his holy honor the bishop had told him, he had become mute in the company of strangers. And now all the world was full of strangers. He had always learned new things quickly and could converse simply in many languages. That was the talent which had given him value, and that was the gift from God that he must now withhold. He communicated with others in signs; he prayed in Greek; he dreamed in Kush, the tongue of his childhood.

Sleep had come easily, for he was weary, and his dreams this night had been restive. It was still a dark moonlit night when he opened his eyes, and he started. A dog was licking his face.

XLII

Like Vivienne, Nicolaos too was wondering where God was in all of this. But for him it was more a puzzle than a question. The answer waited for him, just beyond his dizzy, muddled thoughts. If he could clear his head, surely his mind would mold the prayer that had always brought God near, and with the help of the Holy Spirit he would piece the puzzle. He needed time and rest. His head ached. He felt of his nose. Broken, he was sure. In the darkness he wiped away the blood he could not see as best he could with the hem of his garment.

Seated on the concrete floor, he leaned against a wall that was damp and smelled of mold. Time and rest. It hurt to breathe deeply; his ribs were bruised or broken. And his knees where he had fallen repeatedly smarted still, and were swollen. "So it was with the Christ," he murmured aloud, and found that even speech caused pain, for his lips were torn.

Most hurtful was the uncertainty. He did not know the fate of his priests and deacons, his friends. Had Clodio and his family reached safety? Had Arsenios? And what of stubborn, maddening Deaconess Mena? The children? His uncle Methodius was old and increasingly feeble. He might not be able to bear such abuse as this and live. There had been no word from the Patera See since long before the first edict. Not knowing was a kind of death.

His brain was not working. He could remember seeing the mission a shambles, seeing Alexander taken away. He remembered being hounded to sacrifice to Roman gods; he remembered blows. But how long between arrest and abandonment here in the dark he could not know. How long without food, without water, he could only guess. He would ask his Lord to receive him or to sustain him, as he willed it, when he could think again. For now, only time and rest.

✠

"Bishop? Bishop Nicolaos?"

He opened his eyes to the half-light of dawn and the sight of a bruised and concerned face bending over him. "Alex!"

"I am here," he answered.

"Praise God!"

Alexander left him for a moment to fetch a cup of water to slake his thirst. It was a balm to his parched lips and throat.

"What of the others?"

"I do not know," Alexander said. "Peter and the deaconess were away from the mission when we were seized, Peter on an errand to buy bread and Mena visiting the family that was to assist her."

That much was news. That much was hope.

"She had the babe with her?"

"I am sure of it."

The light was growing somewhat. He could see that one of Alex's eyes was nearly swollen shut. "Are you very much hurt?"

"I will live." The young priest raised a clenched fist, very much the warrior. "So long as they allow it, I will live for Christ. Die for him, if needs be!"

Nicolaos, filled with pride and grief, took a deep breath to stay a dry sob; it still hurt to breathe. As the shadows about them withdrew he could see other forms huddled near them.

"There are many believers here, holy bishop. Many. They need your guidance. I need you."

The cross of holy office. So be it. With all his strength he gathered himself, and as he did the clouds in his mind drifted away, and the words that had never failed him found his lips:

Father, Brother, dearest Friend,

Love that will not—cannot—end:

Help me always keep in mind

I need but ask; Your will, not mine.

I need but listen, strive to see

all the good accorded me.

Help me pray. Help me attend,

Heavenly Father, Brother, Friend.

Amen.

XLIII

What can be said of captivity? One's life is held ensnared, but one's will to live, wholly within his sacred essence, may be nurtured. The body is hapless prisoner; but the mind, by the grace of God, runs free. And what of close confinement? A cloister has welcome walls to keep the world at bay; but a prison seals those inside it from the world and forms its own reality. As Nicolaos himself would tell you, any hardship is merely what you make of it.

It took him weeks, once his wounds had healed and his pain subsided, to find some semblance of order in his new existence. He thanked God and his uncle for the Scriptures long committed to memory, and the trust born of a sweet childhood for the ease with which he addressed his Lord on behalf of those imprisoned with him. They sought his counsel daily and yearned for his ministrations. Buoyed by the faith of these, his people, his new congregation, he prayed for guidance. What he lacked in provisions and holy implements was counterweighed by ingenuity and contrivance. On the first Lord's Day—at least, it was believed to be a Sunday—that he could collect crumbs of hoarded bread and a cup of watered wine to speak the words of consecration over them, the sacrament was more splendid and joyful than that celebrated in the finest cathedral upon plates of gold.

There were many guards and gate keepers, most of them indifferent; but there was one particular Lycian-born ruffian whose curiosity drew him ever closer. And as he overheard more and more of the verbal exchanges between Christians and observed their rituals—which did not, to his amazement, include cannibalism or human sacrifice—his shrewdness made him an ally.

He announced his name one day that had been a long time coming. "I am Timon. I am not without friends in the garrison," he boasted. "What can I do for you, your honor?"

Thus it was that Nicolaos was supplied with a small flask of olive oil which he blessed and could use to anoint the sick and dying. For they did die, these caged souls, many of them, and it was good that he could ease their going. And Timon saw that it was good.

Chaos reigned outside the prison walls, confusion within. With the second edict which had seen Nicolaos and others arrested, properties believed to be Christian holdings had been seized, and livelihoods were subsequently lost among the general population. Roman jails, never intended for long term incarceration, were now overburdened with political prisoners—priests, deacons, lectors, and exorcists—to the extent that dangerous criminals were released in order to make room for them.

In anticipation of the twentieth anniversary of his rule, to be celebrated with great fanfare at Rome in November, Diocletian issued a third edict, one of "clemency." The terms were that any imprisoned clergyman could be freed, so long as he made a sacrifice to the gods. Eager to be rid of the Christians crowding their prisons, jailers happily tortured into submission those who failed to comply, or simply released them, publicly declaring the lie that they had apostatized.

In time Alexander came to his bishop. "I was told that I sacrificed to Apollo and so am to be released in the morning!" His earnest face was lined in anguish, his forehead furrowed with anger or fear. "It is not true! I swear it! I will die rather than leave you here!"

"Nay, nay," Nicolaos exclaimed, "you must go! You must go and keep The Way alive with friends outside these walls. You must be Christ for them, Alex. Think of it. This is your duty, your new call to serve the Lord."

The younger man was desolate, suppressing tears.

"You must go, and go with God. I give you my blessing!"

Nicolaos made the sign of the cross on Alexander's brow, and the two embraced.

Days later, when their ranks had thinned and he understood that Alex was truly gone, he asked Timon why he, Bishop of Myra, had not been tortured further or killed.

"They are afraid of you," Timon shrugged. "They have heard of your deeds, your honor, and they are afraid."

XLIV

A nd so began the long years of imprisonment without the comfort of a well-known face from more carefree days, without true human companionship, without a fellow priest to share the servant burden. The yoke of Christ is easy, Nicolaos reminded himself every day with his morning prayers, because the Lord bears it with me. More than at any time since he was a child made bereft by the loss of his nurse, he relied upon the bond he felt with Jesus. This indignity is no more than my brother Lord bore for me, he thought; nor this pain, nor this. Jesus suffered far more than I, he told himself, to free me from the bondage of sin and secure for me eternal life.

He continued to minister to his fellow prisoners when allowed to mingle with them, and to share the Word just as he shared his food. He grew quite thin and the dampness in his cell troubled his knees. In time his beard reached his breast and he could see that it was streaked with gray. News from outside the walls was scarce and discouraging. When he had been locked away for a year, perhaps a little more, there was yet a fourth edict commanding that men, women and children be herded to a public place and be forced to make a collective sacrifice. Those who refused would be executed. Nicolaos subsequently gathered from Timon's infrequent disclosures that sentiment among pagans throughout the empire was turning in favor of those persecuted, particularly after this latest proclamation. There was something about the fortitude with which most Christians bore unimaginable cruelties and accepted a martyr's death that appealed to the populace.

Timon arranged to be present more and more often when Nicolaos spoke to the others about The Way. He made no overt sign that he accepted any of the teachings, but his interest was obvious. When he began bringing bread he had secreted, so that the bishop no longer had to save bits of his own rations for consecration, Nicolaos asked if he believed and wanted to be baptized.

"No, your honor, not now."

"If not now, when?"

"When I have seen you freed by your Jesus god."

"But I am free, Timon."

The man went away shaking his head, unconvinced.

There were days when Clodio felt no less confined than the holy friend he prayed was yet alive in prison. Their underground home was challenging for him, but was near lethal for Vivienne. Their youngest, a boy, had been born undersized and sickly. His wife toiled to care for him and for all of them, and would not or could not shake the melancholy that had descended upon her from the moment they went into hiding. The girl so beguiling and joyful whom he had loved from his youth seemed lost to him now, and he realized with grief and repressed longing that there would be no more children so long as they lived in exile.

He spent his days working wood and metals, carving bowls and small necessities that brought a meager price in the Patera markets but enough to vary their diet of greens and beans with meat. He went above with other men to barter and on one such excursion saw the presbyter Alexander and was able to speak with him in private. Of Peter Alex had no word, only the rumor that a mute black man "drab as any sparrow" was said to be accompanying a Gaulish or Germanic itinerant performing odd tasks for pay throughout the province. Alex asked about the deaconess Mena, but Clodio could tell him only that the child she had sought to save was being cared for.

"Will you not join us, your honor? I can show you the way."

"No," Alexander said. "I am able to serve in concealment here in the city. Those who have been spared know where to find me, and I know them. It is as the bishop willed it. Are there not priests with you?"

"There are two. We have a chapel and do not want for worship."

"Then you are blessed." The young priest bowed his head. "As am I, in fulfilling my duty."

When Clodio told Vivienne about the encounter the hunger in her eyes made him regret sharing his news.

And as though Vivienne's misery were not enough, Clodio would long remember the day he discovered that his son Nicolaos had gone above with some of his young companions.

"I saw birds flying free, Father! Think of it, free to fly away! And the sun so warm and the trees so tall, the sky so blue!"

He had cuffed the boy, and shaken him by the shoulders, much to his later shame. "You must not, Nicolaos! You must not do what I have forbidden!"

The hurt in the boy's eyes was heartbreaking. "But why, Father? Why, when the Lord's world is so beautiful?"

"Because you must make your own beauty here, my son, because there are dangers above, from those who claim the world as their own and will not allow you any part of it. You must make our life here below beautiful, for your mother, for all of us, until it is safe to return above. Promise me!"

The boy gave his word, he would not venture above again without permission; and the man felt crushed beneath the weight of it.

XLV

All unknown to Nicolaos, there were forces at work in the world which would alter the course of his life and the very future of all believers in The Way. In the year 274, when Nico was a four-year-old child learning at the knee of his Nonna, a cherished son was born to a Greek Christian woman of Anatolia called Helena and the Roman soldier Constantius Chlorus, who would later become one of the four rulers of the Tetrarchy. After rising in military ranks to praetorian prefect of Gaul, when their son Constantine was approaching manhood, Constantius left Helena to marry the stepdaughter of Caesar Maximian.

Young Constantine would receive a broad education in the court of Diocletian at Nicodemia, serve with his father in the Roman army in the West, and through various political machinations become his father's heir to power, and eventually emperor of all Rome. Throughout shifts in fortune, position and favor, however, Constantine would remain loyal to his beloved Christian mother Helena; and while demonstrating devotion to the Roman sun god for most of his life, he would be respectfully open to the tenets of Christianity.

On May 1, 305, both Diocletian and Maximian abdicated. Constantius and Galerius became senior emperors. The persecutions and harsh edicts continued. Constantine succeeded his father on July 25, 306, and immediately made declarations ending persecutions and restoring to Christians what they had lost.

And so the climate outside the prison walls was changing, while existence inside them remained chillingly the same. Nicolaos heard in time of the generosity of Constantine in the West, countered by further cruelties ordered by the leaders in the East. Even as Galerius, co-author with Diocletian of the Great Persecution, rescinded all former orders with an Edict of Toleration upon his deathbed in 311, his successor Maximinus Daza renewed persecutions in the Eastern provinces with a vengeance. It was a dizzying, confusing era to those who were privy to the ever changing news of Roman proclamations and civil wars.

For Nicolaos, often despondent yet never quite despairing, striving to remain constant and loving to fellow sufferers, to be challenging but grateful to the grizzled and resistant pagan Timon, the dictum of these slow, agonizing years was clear: Jesus, I trust in you.

XLVI

It was a day of uncommon sunshine. Or perhaps it was merely that the sun had been denied him for so long. His eyes hurt with the joy of it, so that he shaded them with a trembling hand.

"Your day has come, your honor," said Timon, "and happy I am to see it." His jailer had one more bag of bread for him, one small jug of wine that this time was not diluted. He pressed these gifts upon Nicolaos and bent his stubborn pagan head for a blessing that was freely given. "You have friends waiting, I think."

Beyond the prison gate three anxious figures stood beneath a plane tree. It took a moment for the dim uncertainty of many years to be pushed away by the thrill of recognition. The tallest man stepped forward first, a grinning Clodio paler than Nicolaos remembered, and made old before his time; secondly a now bearded Alexander, thin and eager and bright eyed; and lastly Arsenios, gray and bent with age but thankful, he declared, to behold "the young master" once again.

"God be praised, for He is good," exclaimed Nicolaos, embracing one man after another. "I had hoped . . ." He could not finish; he was overcome with deep feeling.

"We have a cart and mule," Clodio said, "to take you and Arsenios into Myra." He took the jug and sack of bread and led his friend to the cart in which rugs had been laid to ease the shocks of the journey. "Just a short descent from these rocky hills, and then the way is smooth."

And so they set out, the two younger men leading the mule or walking beside the conveyance, taking care to follow the path least rugged. Nicolaos breathed in the fresh air, gazed in wonder at the greenery, at the blue of the sky, at the birds overhead, and found it all beautiful; he could not get enough.

"You will find much changed," Clodio was saying, "yet much that is the same. A few of us have already undertaken the cleaning and repairing of your church-house, Sea Turtle, for little but the shell remains."

"Sea Turtle?" asked Alexander.

Clodio was laughing. Nicolaos felt a wetness in his eyes. His heart was about to burst with gladness. "It is nothing," he explained when he found words, "a childhood name given me by a young Scorpion."

Clodio nodded proudly and looked at his friend with genuine love. "It is nothing, and yet it is everything."

A day of sunshine so bright that it watered the eyes.

Clodio told him many things on the journey to the city, many things. How with the lessening of abuses in the nearer areas of Anatolia, many of those in hiding locally had begun to venture forth. How he had heard that his uncle the Bishop Methodius had been seized before he could go to one of the many other cave villages in the hills; the rumor was that he had been tried as an enemy of Rome and had been transported to Tyre[75]. How the Roman army was garrisoned in the yellow house on the Patera cliffs. "For that reason," Clodio said, "when we decided to come above we traveled east to Myra." He looked away self-consciously. "And of course we hoped to collect you when you were finally released."

"What is it, Clodio?" Nicolaos asked, sensing more to the story. "What is troubling you?"

---

75 ancient city of Phoenicia Libani, Roman Diocese of Oriens; modern day Tyre, Lebanon

He hesitated, then "It is Vivienne," he said at last. "You will find her much changed." He hung his head sadly. "Our third child, little Enos, did not live. He was small and sickly from birth, and did not thrive. Before he had been with us two years, he was taken with a fever."

Nicolaos reached over the side of the cart to catch Clodio's shoulder. "My friend," he murmured. Clodio covered his friend's hand with his own and held it for a long moment as he walked on.

"It was hard for all of us," he continued. "Young Nicolaos was rebellious and angry. Our little Irene had doted on her baby brother and could not be consoled. But Vivienne—" He looked up with desperation in his eyes. "Vivienne was never accepting of our arrangement, our life underground. And after Enos, it was—it was as though she died with him."

XLVII

All that Clodio had told him had not quite prepared him for the reality of his return. By the time they reached the city and had traversed its depth to the wharf district a pale moon was risen and the mists off the sea shrouded the streets in mystery. He could not help but find it reminiscent of the night he had come to the doors of the cathedral, fresh from the Holy Land, and had been confronted by the call to his future. One muted light glowed softly ahead, and as they drew nearer became a beacon; it was a lantern placed in the window of his cathedral. When Alexander pulled the heavy doors open it seemed the whole of his past and all the prospect of that yet to come were met inside, in the glorious light of a dozen more lanterns and twice as many stout candles.

Vivienne was there, and the children, and faces he remembered from the assembly and mission and many more who were new, all smiling welcome and all talking at once. The tapestry banners were long gone, as well as the wood carvings above what had once served as the altar. But there was the beginning of a fine wooden cross to be finished and polished, and a new altar was waiting to be embellished and dedicated, facing the East. The entire floor had been scraped to its foundation and in the corners were piles of new little tiles to be laid in shades of blue and gold and silver.

"A mosaic floor," Clodio said with pride, "in patterns worthy of our Lord and his people. It will take time, but it will be done."

There were tables in the center of the great vaulted room, laid with white cloths, jugs and plates of foodstuffs covered with napkins.

"We have sausages!" one of the children exclaimed. "And cider and wine!"

"Sausages, imagine that!" said Nicolaos.

Vivienne brought her children forward, young Nicolaos a strapping lad of twelve or thirteen, and Irene, looking the very picture of Vivienne when he had first seen her in her mother's courtyard garden.

"And this is Joseph," Clodio said, his arm about a boy nearly as tall as his son. "He and your namesake are inseparable, much as you and I were at their age."

"The child born at the mission," Alex offered.

Nicolaos looked at the youngster, fair haired and hazel eyed, and felt a stir of recognition. "Zelle's child."

"Mena's boy," the lad corrected, for he had long heard the stories of the woman who had saved his life.

"And the deaconess?" Nicolaos asked.

Alexander shook his head.

Vivienne busied herself with the food, uncovering the platters of sausages, the pickled eggs, the olives and brined cucumbers and leeks, the bread, and last of all the fruit and sweet pastries. The bishop was thin, terribly thin for a man his size. It would take the cooking of all the women devoted to the church, and much uninterrupted rest, to restore his body. She wondered what it would take to restore his mind. Surely, she thought, to be locked away for so long, longer even than she and her family had lived underground, surely he must have felt abandoned by his God. "His" God, she mused, for she was no longer sure of Him herself. Too much had happened; too much loss, too much suffering. Clodio was stalwart in his commitment to The Way, but Clodio had not had a part of himself ripped away. He had not held their child to his breast, begging God to save him. She was sure her husband's injury, his grief, was not the same; she lived her own every hour of every day.

At the corner of her eye she observed the bishop approaching her, and she felt a thrill of fear. She did not want to be confronted, and she did not wish to pretend.

"Vivienne," he said softly.

She raised her eyes to his and found them warm and moist with compassion.

"Vivienne," he said again. "I ask for your blessing."

She looked at him dumbly.

He said it again: "I ask for your blessing. I have no mother to commend my work, to put a benediction upon my head. But you—you have given life and have nurtured life, and like the Mother of our Lord Jesus, you have withstood unspeakable sorrow. I would be honored." He bowed low before her.

Something wrenched at her heart. An intake of breath very like a sob rocked her very being. She reached out and lay her hand upon his head, graying now.

"The peace and love of God be upon you," she said after a moment. And she believed the words.

XLVIII

And so his work continued. The family of Clodio made a home in the mission near the church where the Deaconess Mena had worked, carrying on their ministry much as they had at the yellow house in Patara. Joseph lived with them, as well as several other orphans or families decimated by the years of persecution. Arsenios lived in chambers within the church house occupied by the bishop and Alexander, and managed the assembly's finances with a nimble finesse that belied his years. "You shall have it," was his frequent pronouncement when confronted with a need, and magically the funds needed for building or for charity appeared. Nicolaos himself went out to the people, visiting the streets throughout his see much as he had before "the interruption," as he referred to his incarceration. Within a few months the congregation assembled at the cathedral to hear him preach each Lord's Day had swelled, even as the mosaic tiles were slowly installed, painting a growing pattern of faith beneath their very feet.

Gradually good health was restored to him, and he began to feel as sound in body as in mind and spirit. Only when word reached him that Methodius had been executed in Tyre did his fortitude falter. An enormous wave of guilt accompanied his considerable grief, for he had survived the worst of the persecution relatively unscathed while his dear uncle and mentor had been sacrificed. When he agonized aloud over "Why?" Alexander responded with compassion.

"I think because of his writings," he said. "Your uncle never stopped writing. He was   known throughout the world for his letters and written works, and not merely within the Christian community."

"That is true."

"Your service, if I may say," Alex continued, "has thus far been all action. You are known not for written words which may be preserved and used against you but for wondrous and generous deeds; for preaching and counseling that is not set down but which your people take to heart."

"Perhaps."

"Also, if I may be so bold, the Bishop Methodius had served long and well; his race was run. It may be that the Lord has further plans for you."

Nicolaos considered all of this, but it did little to lessen the sorrow he felt. So many good people lost to the world, not least among them his parents, brave unselfish Mena, the child Enos, his Uncle Methodius. So many precious souls to carry with him, so many to live for, that their roles in God's plan be not forgotten. It was a burden he was thankful to share with his divine Friend, who in due time would make it lighter.

XLIX

He saw them approaching even before they appeared to notice him. A tall black man, thin and wiry, a much shorter, muscular blonde fellow, and a large dog, brown and shaggy, with lolling tongue. He was on one of his walkabouts through the marketplace, accosted on all sides by those in need, true beggars and solace seekers alike, loud in their supplication for coins or blessings. At first he doubted his eyes, for this was something he had longed for since returning to Myra, and the seeking heart plays tricks upon the mind. But when the black man sighted him and broke into laughter, there was no doubt.

"Can it be? Peter, my friend!"

"Your honor!"

They grasped each other by the forearms, examining faces, then fell into an embrace. The dog went immediately to Nicolaos, nuzzling his legs.

"Pelz!" cried Peter's companion, "No! Come!"

"All is well," Nicolaos assured him, bending to give the dog his attention for a moment, caressing his ears. He turned to the people gathered near and made a sweeping sign of the cross over their heads. "Forgive me! I must welcome an old friend!"

The crowd disbursed as the bishop turned back to the two newcomers.

Peter lay a hand on the shorter man's shoulder. "This is Emil. I have traveled with him many a year."

"God's peace be upon you, Emil. You must eat with me this day, both of you. And Pelz, is it?"

The dog wagged its tail.

"We will make a celebration! Alexander will be overjoyed to see you, Peter! Make haste, come!"

✠

Alexander was overjoyed indeed. He made their guests comfortable with cushioned seats at a table soon laid with roast fowl and fresh crusty bread, grapes and two kinds of cheese, hard and soft. The dog settled on his own clean rug dignified with a water bowl and marrow bone.

"I heard reports, Peter, and dared hope they were of you," Alex exclaimed.

Peter nodded. "Even holding back speech and keeping to the shadows, I am a conspicuous figure," he said with some pride. "Conspicuous, have I the right word?"

"Indeed," said Nicolaos. He studied his friend, finding comfort in the familiar deep voice and good-humored manner. Peter was as nimble and quick-witted as ever. His face bore a decade's lines and furrows and his hair was silvered in places, but he was the same Black Peter. "And your music?"

"I carried my flute with me always and learned to play songs common to the western provinces, but only in private among friends."

"His music was the bond that kept us together," his companion said. There was fondness in Emil's blue eyes. "I have no talent myself, so I appreciate Peter's the more." He spoke with a thick Germanic accent; "Peter" became "Beetah" in his mouth. He scratched the fair stubble on his chin thoughtfully. "Pelz and I, we fell to sleep many a night listening to the pan flute."

Nicolaos regarded the dog, whose ears perked at his name. "Pelz, what does that mean?"

"Fur," Emil said simply. "His coat is not usual, no?"

It was true. The shaggy fur was mottled in several discordant shades of brown and was oddly curly; it gave the dog a winsome look about the face.

"How did you and Peter find each other?"

Emil grinned, and with a stout finger traced the sign of the fish on the table. "Peter played the mute in company, but when he was alone with me he showed me that he had some of the words of my people, and some of the Gaul as well as the Greek. And a tune he played, I had heard before among Christians. A man so learned and well-traveled is either rich—which he was not—or hunted." He popped a grape into his mouth. "Together we were a useful curiosity. Each alone was a target."

"Emil is a skilled metalworker," Peter said, "and I apply myself to any labor. As a team we worked for little pay, or for a roof, and then we moved on."

"But you will stay with us, I hope?" Nicolaos asked.

Peter brightened, and looked to his friend.

"If you have need of a smith," Emil said.

"Absolutely! Our church and mission must be rebuilt." Nicolaos gazed with affection at Black Peter. "And as ever, I am in need of an assistant with three languages."

"More than three, now!" Peter exclaimed.

"Then it is decided!" Alexander said. "We have rooms here that are not being used. I will show you to them after we eat."

The bishop blessed the food, whereupon all four beings set to with enthusiasm, some bread and bits of fowl discreetly dropping to the floor.

L

It seemed that during those seasons of relative freedom[76] when more and more groups of Christians reappeared in their midst miraculously—from whence Roman governors could not learn—that the gods of heaven and earth seemed intent on punishing the eastern provinces for failure to keep those wanton disbelievers in check. Caelus, god of the sky, as well as Jupiter and Tempestas, god and goddess of storms, were called upon to send much needed rain. Growers prayed to Ceres and Saturn for the good harvest that eluded them, and those in government desperately besieged the god Consus to protect grain storage. Sacrifices were made to Sol Invictus, god of the sun, in hopes the relentless heat would abate. And while the Greeks among them appealed to Cronus, their god of agriculture, those in power who possessed at least a passing understanding of farming made reckless promises to Sors, the Roman god of luck.

In his cathedral and in the streets and on his knees in his chamber at night, Nicolaos prayed, "Lord God, you know our need. The land is parched, the harvests few. In your mercy please send rain to the land, even as you rain your love upon our hearts that we may accept your will."

The drought continued into its third year, and there was famine.

---

76 310-312 A.D.

Clodio pushed away the lock of hair falling into his eyes with a hand that smelled of fish. He must ask Vivienne to cut his hair, for it was bothersome when it grew long. He smiled at the thought, for he knew that she would not only do as he asked, she would also bathe his head and neck with cool scented water and kiss away the throbbing in his head that always tormented him when he worked too long in the sun. He was mending his nets.

Odd the turn his life had taken. At first he had somewhat resented Emil, the itinerant from Germania. As a metalworker he lacked artistry but made up for that with industry, and he was a fair carpenter as well. The work on the church had moved forward quickly with his help. But Emil had no family to provide for, and Clodio did. After the homecoming of his holy friend the bishop, his wife had slowly returned to him; not quite the laughing bride of their youth, but a loving companion. She was with child again, and he would do anything to keep that haunted lost look from her eyes.

When the bishop walked the city now the beggars did not want coins, for what could they buy? They wanted bread. No rain, no crops. No crops, no feed for the animals. There was little grain for bread, less meat and milk, fewer grapes for wine. The one source of sustenance the drought did not curb was the sea. Arsenios had provided the price of a small skiff. Young Nicolaos and Joseph helped him, and while there were disappointing days, most weeks he and his boys caught enough fish and mollusks to feed the mission and the men at the church. Black Peter roamed the markets and traded for herbs and spices that made even the most meager catch more than palatable.

The Lord had worked a miracle, Clodio reflected; he was a fisherman at last. But it was an odd turn.

Nicolaos had a recurring dream. He was back on the cliffs below the Patara lighthouse in suffocating heat, alone and hungry. There was a sense of urgency, for his parents were waiting for him in the yellow house, and they were weak and needed food more than he. Again and again he dug for roots or snails or for any edible thing, but always the sand ran from his empty hands. He prayed and called out to his God until finally the birds of the air, warblers and bee-eaters, took pity upon him and dipped low to stir the hot air with their wings. There was no manna from heaven, but at least he could breathe. And he would ever wake with a presentiment of blessing yet to come.

LI

Hunger proved to be an enemy more perilous than power. Starvation drives men to madness, and madness to capitulation. Rome could have gained pagan converts among the population of Lycia, even among some aspirant Christians, had Rome offered food. The most vulnerable, the elderly and the very young, were dying at a frightening rate, while Nicolaos besieged heaven on behalf of his neighbors of all religions. He also observed that the collapse of faith and hope along with loss of life was not the only danger. Men denied nourishment tend to violence while there is strength left in them, for their motivation is survival. It was a volatile time.

Thus it was alarming yet not surprising when Clodio's son burst into the church at the height of a summer's day, flushed and breathless.

"My father asks that you come quickly! Two ships have docked, filled with grain, but they are stopping here only for supplies. A crowd gathers, and he fears bloodshed!"

Again, as once before, an unseemly sprint to the wharf in his altar vestments, with curious onlookers following. The tall masts of the ships were visible against the cloudless sky even before they rounded a turn and began the descent to the quayside. "Where is Joseph?" Nicolaos shouted.

"With my father. See! There they wait for you!"

Indeed, Clodio and Joseph were standing near the mooring of the first of a pair of very large corbitas. "They are taking grain from Alexandria[77] to Byzantium,[78] both of them," Clodio called, his face set like a mask of despair.

---

77 city in Egypt
78 later called Constantinople, now Istanbul, Türkiye

Nicolaos nodded and hurried not to the nearer ship but to the other. On its bow a soaring bird was painted.

He made his way to the gangway of the second ship with Clodio, young Nicolaos and Joseph in tow. The crowd parted to allow them to pass, their questioning murmur becoming strident.

From the deck a benevolently smiling man with an unmistakable air of authority watched them board. "Bishop Nicolaos!"

"Peace be unto you."

"And you!" The smile became wider, bright white even teeth striking in a darkly ruddy face. The man tugged at his beard. "It is I, Georgios!" he exclaimed. "Do you not know me? The voyage to Caesarea Maritima, your honor!"

"Aye! Georgios of Patera!"

The man nodded vigorously, clearly pleased. "I am now whiskered," he pronounced, "and I have risen in the world, as have you. I am master of this ship."

"Then God be praised, for He has surely brought you to us."

The captain's face clouded. "We are here with our sister ship only to load supplies, your honor, for the second leg of our journey to Byzantium."

Nicolaos looked out upon the city. "Our people are dying," he said simply. He gestured over the side at the wharf, where the vocal and angry mob was growing. "They are good people, but they are desperate."

"Surely you and your friends do not threaten me, bishop!"

"Certainly not. No one here wishes harm to anyone. But our children are crying with hunger. The children of Patera, Georgios, as well as the sons and daughters of Myra. Our Lord Jesus Christ charged us with feeding the poor, but we are all rendered poor when we have no bread to share."

Georgios shook his head. "You don't understand, bishop. The grain is not mine to give. It belongs to the leaders of Byzantium. If I offload even part of my cargo here I will answer to them. I will face retribution, lose everything—my ship, perhaps even my life."

"Nay, Georgios," Nicolaos said. "It is you who do not understand. God has sent you to me. I have prayed for this."

Georgios remembered the calming of the storm at sea, how terrified he had been, and how awestruck at the outcome. But it was one thing to witness a miracle, and quite another to be asked to be part of one. He looked at the young boys with Nicolaos. Troubled, earnest, thin as rails. He had such a boy at home.

"What if I were to promise to send full payment for the grain you leave here?" the bishop asked. "I am known in Byzantium, as was my father before me; I think my credit would be accepted."

Dumfounded, Georgios looked this time at Nicolaos, whose soft brown eyes held his until something moved in him and he relented. "Yes."

"Amen!" Nicolaos said. "My friend Clodio here will send to the granary to make arrangements."

Orders were given, instructions laid down. Men who obeyed him without question began setting a plan in motion. The crowd below was noisier, but its attitude was suddenly benign. Already Georgios was feeling something very like regret, a stubborn visceral fear that would not leave his gut until his voyage was over.

"You must come dine with us," the bishop was saying. "We have little, but what we have is yours. Do you like mussels prepared with olive oil and garlic?"

Georgios nodded meekly and allowed himself to be led off his vessel.

"The figure painted on the side of your ship, what manner of bird is it?"

"Why, it is a dove."

The bishop smiled.

Although Georgios dreaded landing at the port of Byzantium with two-thirds of his cargo lacking, when the grain was offloaded and its weight measured, it was exactly the amount recorded when his ship left Alexandria. His cargo master, having witnessed the transfer of grain at Myra and all that had transpired there, asked for verification. But the amount did not change; there was no loss. Lightheaded with relief, Georgios took the promissory letter from Bishop Nicolaos to show the treasury official in Byzantium and explained all that had happened, with his cargo master as witness. The official did not doubt him, for the reputation of Bishop Nicolaos was well known. Upon return home Georgios became a catechumen in The Way and was baptized, along with his wife and his son.

Grain was fairly distributed in Myra and surrounding villages. No family went without. It lasted two seasons until the drought broke, and what remained was scattered as seed to yield a good harvest. People everywhere were talking of this miracle and praising the Christian God. And so it came to pass that Nicolaos of Myra, once lauded as "the Boy Bishop," became known as "Wonderworker," a term unheard in Lycia since the time of Gregory.[79]

---

79 St. Gregory the Wonderworker, 213-270 A.D., Bishop of Neocaesarea

LII

The years that followed the famine miracle were good years. Nicolaos never wavered in thanking his Lord God for favor, for indeed it seemed all he touched as the holy Bishop of Myra was at the pleasure of heaven, and he was supremely happy. His church was rebuilt a thing of beauty, and it was filled daily with good people wishing only to do the will of God. Together they fed and clothed the poor and taught their children and spread the love of Jesus wherever ears could hear and eyes could see.

Clodio, a craftsman again, produced fine furnishings that Lyceans and Romans alike sought out in the marketplace, and with Alexander and Peter he saw the mission grow again and prosper. He and Vivienne welcomed another daughter and then a little son. Even with the care of the household and small children to burden her, Vivienne found time to fashion fine robes for the bishop as "befitting a worker of wonders."

"You shall be eclipsed by me no longer," exclaimed Black Peter, who had resumed his colorful costumes.

"It is too grand," Nicolaos murmured doubtfully, turning this way and that before a mirror of polished tin. It was a coat of crimson trimmed with bands of green embroidery and lined with white lamb's wool.

"Nonsense," said Vivienne, placing a pin where she would sew a tuck in the drapery. "You must look the part," she said, "and you must be warm if you insist on walking this city in winter weather."

The shaggy brown dog at his feet lay back, exposing his belly in hopes of rubs and pounding his tail against the floor.

"See, even Belsnickel approves."

Nicolaos laughed and had to agree. After the Emperor Constantine's Edict of Milan[80] made it legal to practice Christianity and returned confiscated property to Christians and Jews, Emil the metalworker had decided to return to Germania. Disgusted with Pelz, who preferred Nicolaos, he had fiercely exclaimed, "You are no longer my Pelz, you are Pelsnickel. The good bishop is welcome to you, ungrateful cur." But he had cuffed the dog affectionately about the ears and gifted him with a studded leather collar before taking his leave. The dog was known as Belsnickel henceforth, and he approved wholeheartedly of everything Nicolaos did.

They formed a colorful trio, the celebrated bishop, the gaudily garbed musician-ambassador—for it seemed by now that Black Peter spoke every language—and the large brown dog, attracting the faithful and the curious but most of all the children on their jaunts about the city, nearly every Lord's Day. They were good years indeed, and fruitful.

✠

The long anticipated time came finally when a parcel was delivered to Nicolaos, a sheaf of parchments wrapped in linen, bound with string and sealed. Old Arsenios was beside himself with joy and pride.

"It is all here," he told the young master, his bishop, "the title, the conveyances, the letter of reparation."

Nicolaos handled the parchments with fingers that trembled just a bit. "I have prayed for this," he said. "Thank you, good Arsenios, for all your negotiations and hard work."

Arsenios nodded. "God is good," he said.

---

80 February, 313 A.D.

"I wish to see it again, the house of my fathers." It lifted his spirit merely to say the words. "Will you accompany me?"

The old man clasped his hands as though in prayer. "In spirit only," he said. "I shall be content to hear your report when you return."

Nicolaos forgot sometimes that the controller of his accounts was at least a decade older than his father Epiphánios would have been, had he lived. "Just Clodio and I, then," he said, and he could not deny that the prospect excited him.

They formed a colorful trio

LIII

"Was there ever a sight more beautiful?"

Clodio gazed at his friend, whose face was rapt upon the sunset and the shore, clearly enthralled with the view from the ship's rail. "It is a pretty night," he agreed. The sky was afire with red and streaked with clouds of gold; the pale limestone Patara lighthouse and the cliffs and yellow house behind it were brought to brilliance by the sun's dying rays.

"Never before have I beheld this approach from the water," Nicolaos said. "When I left for the Holy Land I traveled overland to Myra and embarked from there."

"I remember."

"The same sea, the same homeland, and yet this is so far superior!"

"It is the beach," Clodio said simply, ever logical. "At Myra are stout gray rocks and the piers of industry, as though man carved a port out of angry stone walls. Here we have the good sand beaches."

"It is more than that."

"Oh, aye." His friend was seeing their childhood, the home he had loved, the tombs of his own parents and Clodio's father, brother and mother-in-law beneath the little church by the sea. He was seeing all that was no longer there.

While they watched, the nightly flame burst forth atop the lighthouse, as though welcoming them home.

Their ship put in by torchlight at the commercial wharf nearest the arched city gate and the sad old toppled head of Apollo. Having chosen a taberna that offered meals as well as a clean bed, they settled in for a cena fit for seafarers.

"No! No fish," Clodio told the server, who offered to bring a salver of freshly caught sea bass.

"Have you a hearty meat stew of some kind?" asked Nicolaos. "Lamb perhaps? Or fowl, fowl will do. And bread, plenty of bread." He grinned at Clodio after the server left their table. "I fear you do not appreciate one of God's true miracles, old land Scorpion. 'God said, Let the water teem with an abundance of living creatures.'[81] And the sea brought forth life to sustain us."

Clodio returned his friend's grin and winked. "I thank Him every day, O learned Sea Turtle, for his great variety of sustenance, and for hands that are not mine to pull his fish from the sea."

The server brought stale barley bread and crumbly white cheese floating in oil, followed by steaming bowls of pottage vaguely suggestive of mutton. "Sustenance," Nicolaos observed wryly, raising an eyebrow.

Their conversation turned somber after their hunger had been satisfied. "I do not know what we will see tomorrow," Nicolaos said. "I understand that the house was ill-used by Rome. It may need a great deal of work."

Clodio nodded. "Arsenios says there are funds to restore it, if needed."

"Are you still determined to stay in Myra? The house is yours again, if you want it."

"I have talked this over with Vivienne, and we are agreed. The yellow house is tied in her mind to the plague deaths and the great persecution and our flight to the underground. Myra is the place of new beginnings."

Nicolaos nodded his understanding.

"It is settled, then. I will make a gift of it to the Patera See, and the bishop may use it as he wills."

---

81 Genesis 1, 29, NAB

"You are generous as always, my friend."

"I am fortunate," Nicolaos said humbly. "It is easy to have a generous heart when the heart is full."

LIV

The soldiers garrisoned in the yellow house had been hard on it indeed, and time's decay had taken its toll as well. It was evident that horses or other livestock had been kept in Johanna's once lovely courtyard. A liquid amber tree and a resilient, determined tamarisk were all that remained of the shade and beauty Nicolaos remembered. Some of the rooms inside on both levels had been defaced with graffiti, and nearly all were in need of new plaster.

"The roof must be replaced, and the stairways need repair," he reflected aloud. "Many tiles in the bath are broken."

Clodio appeared more dismayed than he. "Aye, it is a crime," he exclaimed, "that such a fine house should be treated contemptuously! Yet another abuse by Rome."

"Men behave badly when they know no better," Nicolaos responded mildly. He picked up a twisted piece of iron that had come from the missing courtyard gate. "And when they are far from home and all that is familiar to them." He turned the iron piece in his hands, examining it thoughtfully. "Our Lord tells us that we should pray for those who would insult us or harm us."

Clodio snorted, but held his tongue.

"Come, sit."

They found a place near the old tamarisk that offered a broad stone bench. They sat in silence. Nicolaos gazed long at the house and then out to sea, and Clodio realized that once again that his friend was seeing not with his eyes but with his memory.

"I have spoken with the Bishop of Patara," Nicolaos said at last. "This place will be a sanctuary again, and it will belong to the people."

"Yes. That is good."

"Will you, Clodio, or will one of your friends, fashion a new gate?"

"Of course."

"And will you forge the iron embellishments in the shapes of emblems of our faith? The anchor, the cross?"

"Of course."

The bishop grinned. "And the fish?"

"Absolutely," laughed Clodio, "for the world to see."

Nicolaos clapped an arm about Clodios shoulder. "For the world to see." he echoed. "Think of it! To worship the Christ in the open without hindrance, without persecution. The possibilities are endless. We are so blessed to have lived to see it."

LV

The newfound freedom of religion was exalting to many, and intoxicating to a few. In time Nicolaos came to believe that the sacred liberty to think and speak and worship without fear of consequences led to the sin of pride in some of his brother presbyters. A hot wind of heresy was blowing from the south, toxic and dry as desert dust. He did his best to keep it from invading his see and withering his people; but with every year it became more difficult to defend Christ as true man and true God and to uphold the testimony of the apostles.

It didn't help that he was growing older. He felt his age an encumbrance, much as he was grateful for his life spared and his health preserved. He was moving a bit more slowly, feeling more pain in the joints that had been injured during his captivity, needing more rest than was available to him. Often he found himself responding gruffly—despite his best intentions—when he was challenged, which seemed frequent of late.

"I am saying only that it is logical to question Scripture and to consider the writings of Arius,[82] which may have merit," Joseph said.

"Logic has its uses," the bishop countered. "But logic is merely a path to truth. For my part, I find it logical to accept that which was reported by the men who knew the Lord when he walked among us, who heard the Word from his lips, who saw him transfigured, witnessed him risen, and beheld him ascending to the Father. It is not for us to interpret, twist, add to or change their testimony, but to accept it in faith."

---

82 Cyrenaic (Libyan) presbyter and ascetic educated in Antioch

Joseph clenched his fists in frustration and glared at the floor. He was an earnest young man now of considerable stature; comely with his light eyes and hair and a Roman nose. His quick temper was also a Roman trait, Nicolaos suspected.

"If Jesus was created," Joseph continued stubbornly, "it follows that he is not eternal and is therefore an underling, subject to the rule of God—"

"Not created, begotten! Begotten, not made, just as you were begotten. Or I."

Joseph shook his head. "John's Scripture tells us that Jesus himself said, 'The Father is greater than I'. . ."[83]

"While he was man living among us."

". . . meaning that he is not in fact God, equal to the Father."

"Enough!" Nicolaos brought his own fist down upon the parchments Joseph had brought to him. "I will not hear blasphemy! I know the writings of Arius; they are not new to me. And I tell you they are heretical."

The young man stared hard at the bishop, his color rising, but took a moment to collect himself.

Nicolaos drew a long breath to calm himself as well. "John also said, 'In the beginning was the Word, and the Word was in God's presence, and the Word was God' . . . and 'The Word became flesh and made his dwelling among us.'"[84]

Joseph hung his head. "Did you never question?" he asked softly.

"Never," Nicolaos said, without hesitation. "I have known the Lord Jesus as my friend and savior since I was a small child, and I have accepted all that was taught to me about him." He laid a hand over his heart. "I would know it here if it were not true."

Joseph smiled faintly. "But my mind rules my heart."

---

83 John 14:28 NAB
84 John 1:1, 14 NAB

"And your mind is tested, yes. I understand that. It is natural. I can only advise you to pray on it. Speak to Jesus as you would to me or to Clodio or Peter or to anyone you count as friend. Ask him to guide you, Joseph." He grasped the young man's shoulder affectionately. "And then listen."

"And if I still question?"

"Then I will not ordain you as a presbyter."

Joseph nodded, understanding. Nicolaos watched him walk away, dejected as a beaten pup. Why could not Joseph be like Clodio's sons, finding peace in The Way and contentment in professions like fishing and carpentry? Why must he be drawn to priesthood, yet at war with it? He sensed Mena's disappointment in his counsel of her boy and felt her reproach as surely as if her spirit had been in the room with them, watching with dark eyes from beneath her veil.

LVI

Nicolaos was not alone in the belief that the writings of Arius were heresy. While still a deacon Arius had sided with Meletius of Lycopolis in refusing re-admittance to the Church for those who had repented of denying the faith under fear of Roman torture. For that he had been excommunicated by Bishop Peter of Alexandria. Peter's successor Bishop Achillas re-admitted Arius to Christian communion, however, and made him a presbyter of the Baucalis district of the Alexandrian See. Thus encouraged, Arius had continued propounding his theological views. Perhaps aided by his appearance of ascetic purity and polished charm, his opinions had found support in many quarters. By the year 320 Alexander, the latest Bishop of Alexandria, frustrated with the spread of Arianism, had called a synod[85] of the entire See of Alexandria and its neighboring See of Maerotis, 80 church leaders in all. The end result was a signed document declaring Arianism heretical. Undeterred, Arius had continued to write and teach. Alexander called a council of the entire church in 321, which was attended by 100 leaders. When Arius appeared before them to argue that Jesus the Son was not of the same essence as God the Father, the council was largely scandalized and excommunicated him again.

Arius then went to Palestine, where some bishops supported him. His followers were beginning to resort to violence. The Roman Emperor at that time, Licinius I, wrote to Bishop Alexander and to Arius, asking them to make peace. The contentious confusion continued. Eusebius of Nicomedia convened an independent counsel to consider Arius's views and the actions

---

85 a meeting of clergy, sometimes including laity

taken against him, and the bishops who participated readmitted him to the church. Alexander then summoned yet another council. The attendees agreed that Arius was still excommunicated.

By this time the Emperor Constantine, later called The Great, had come to power as sole ruler[86] of all Rome. He favored Christianity above other religions—which he also tolerated—offering his patronage to the faith embraced by his mother Helena. He hoped to use this rapidly growing religion as a means of achieving unity within his empire. Sensing an ally, Arius complained directly to the emperor.

Constantine invited Arius to make his case before the entire Church at the city of Nicaea[87] in the spring of 325. He formally invited all of the 1,800 Christian bishops throughout both the Roman Empire and the Sassanid Empire.[88] Each bishop was permitted to bring with him two priests and three deacons. Attending bishops would be given free travel to and from their episcopal sees, as well as free lodging.

Nicolaos received his invitation with a degree of eagerness. He had not traveled as far as Nicaea since his voyage to the Holy Land. It would be good to see the lands of Bithynia north of Lycia, and even better to put right the dissention caused by Arianism.

He reached down from his chair to stroke Belsnickel, snoring at his feet. The dog's rough brown coat was shot with gray now, especially on his muzzle. His own beard was silver-white. They were aging together, and since finding each other had never been parted. It would be difficult to leave Bels behind,

---

86 from 324 A.D.
87 modern day Iznik, Türkiye
88 Iranian or Neo-Persian Empire, 224 – 651 A.D.

even for just a few weeks. No matter. This Council of Nicaea was surely a good thing. He would see it through.

The Emperor Constantine appeared to be a friend to Christianity, or at least not its enemy. But Nicolaos, like his father Epiphános, was wary of largesse on the part of any Roman ruler. He would take with him only two companions, his trusted presbyter Alexander and—against his better judgment—the deacon Joseph.

LVII

Because the council was to convene in May, they set out in mid-April to make the trip overland in a private carpentum [89] pulled by two mules. The vehicle was roomy even with three persons inside; and the ride, aided by metal and leather suspension, was surprisingly comfortable. Alexander found traveling tedious and was pleasantly companionable but spent most of his days in silent prayer. Joseph was excited to see Arius in person and hear him speak; he passed his days in sober contemplation, wisely keeping his exhilaration to himself. For Nicolaos the trip was an adventure, an opportunity to experience more of God's vast world and to make friends for Jesus along the way. He was surprised at how well he himself was known, for at every wayside or inn they were received with delight. Blessings and the favor of prayers were asked of the holy Bishop Nicolaos of Myra, and in turn he asked the people he met to pray for him.

They made their way northward at a leisurely yet steady pace, for their driver was skilled and knew the route well. They passed rivers and waterfalls, fields of wild orchids, distant mountains still hoarding snow. They skirted Lake Burdur, known to be salt as the sea, and though they were far inland, saw great congregations of shore birds on the land and in the air. They witnessed bears waking to the spring and heard what could only be the roar of lions coming from the forest. They were enchanted by a liquid amber plantation, beautiful and aromatic. By the time they reached the arched south gate at the walled city of Nicaea, all three travelers were sated with sights and travel weary.

---

89 four-wheeled vehicle with a wooden arched rooftop

The bastioned city of Nicaea was situated at the eastern end of beautiful Lake Askania[90], where the town was fortified with stone walls more than
twice the height of a man and in most places at least 16 feet thick, interspersed
with similarly formidable turrets. Nonetheless, having arrived well in advance
of the council's opening day, Nicolaos was able to secure rooms for himself,
Alexander and Joseph in a two-storied taberna on a hill that afforded a fine
view of the water. Their first order of business in their temporary abode was
prayer, the second food, the third rest. And as a new day dawned they set
about exploring the city.

Many other bishops and patriarchs, presbyters, deacons and acolytes
were arriving by the emperor's invitation. Most had availed themselves of his
generosity with public funds, traveling in large parties. It was easy to see that
by the start of the council the clergy and their entourage would number in
the hundreds, perhaps near 2,000. His holiness Pope Sylvester was unable to
attend but had sent two legates from Rome, Vitus and Vincentius, and would
himself review all decisions made by the council. Other delegates from Italia,
indeed from all over Europe, Africa and Asia, were gathering in numbers so
great that the assembly would be moved from its original proposed site, the
church and necropolis[91] outside the southwestern walls, to the great hall of
Constantine's palace within the city.

In a matter of days the streets, tabernae, baths and markets were teeming with a variety of strange faces and voices: swarthy men, bearded men,
venerable men who bore the scars of persecution. Men who created a genuine Babel, speaking in unfamiliar languages; for although the business of the
council would be conducted in Greek and Latin, among the throngs in the
marketplace men spoke freely in their mother tongues. Even Peter, Nicolaos

---

90 now called Lake Iznik
91 cemetery

reflected, would be challenged to comprehend them all. He and Alexander found respite from crowds and confusion beyond the walls in the quiet coolness of the church or at the lakeside. To amuse the populace while their city was swollen with pious visitors the officials of Nicaea had opened athletic games in its amphitheater. Given his youth, it was not surprising that Joseph was drawn to the games. What surprised Nicolaos was that he did not return from them alone.

Finding Nicolaos and Alexander in the common room of their taberna, Joseph appeared to be well pleased with himself in his choice of companion. The young man with him, only slightly older, carried himself with dignity and humility.

"This is Athenasius,[92] assistant to Bishop Alexander of Alexandria. He has a great desire to speak with you, Holy Bishop."

"The peace of the risen Christ be with you," Nicolaos said.

"And with you," the young man replied.

"Come! You must refresh yourselves in our chambers and break bread with us."

---

92 Athenasius the Great, c. 296-298 – 373, saint and doctor of the church

LVIII

A small repast was sent up to their rooms overlooking the blue Askania. They seated themselves near the windows, so that they might enjoy a pleasant breeze blowing off the lake, and they blessed their food.

"Athenasius is a deacon, like me. He has been charged by his bishop with a great responsibility, to keep a written record of all that transpires at the council," Joseph said. He added eagerly, "What will be my role, bishop? With what am I tasked?"

Amused, Nicolaos said, "To observe and to learn. Why not allow Athenasius to speak for himself?"

Somewhat chagrined, Joseph stoppered his mouth with a morsel of roast lamb and nodded to his new friend.

"I am come because I have heard of your great deeds," Athenasius said. "Indeed, all who survived the famine have heard of Nicolaos of Myra."

"Not my deeds," countered Nicolaos, "but God's. If the Holy Spirit has worked through me, it is because of his mercy and love for all his people. I am an unworthy instrument, but if I can be a sign of God's goodness, my life has meaning."

This answer satisfied their guest. They ate and drank in silence for a few minutes, the younger men exhibiting a wholesome appetite.

"You are not yet ordained a presbyter, then?" asked Alexander.

"I am not. But with the grace of God, that will follow," Athenasius said, "for I believe I have been destined for a life of service to our Church."

"How so?"

Athenasius smiled. "One of my earliest memories comes to mind. I was a small boy, playing with my mates in the sand on the seashore. We were imitating the rite of baptism, and I of course—" his smile grew broader "—played the part of the officiant. Bishop Alexander himself saw us from his window; it was on a spring day such as this. He called us to him. After questioning me he told us that the baptisms were genuine. Both the form and the matter of the sacrament had been valid through my recitation of the proper words and the administration of living water. I was cautioned not to repeat my performance, however, because my playmates were not appropriately catechized."

"Extraordinary!" exclaimed Alex.

"The bishop also invited us to prepare for clerical careers. I alone took his words to heart."

Nicolaos felt a kindred warmth for the young man. "I too felt called at an early age. I have always understood what the Lord desired of me, and have striven to please him."

Joseph, having had his fill of food and of sentiment, pushed away from the table. "There is more that you have in common, is there not?" This prompt directed at their guest.

"Yes," Athenasius said, "I was telling Joseph that like you, I was born to wealth. Not to the aristocracy, not to high position, but to abundance and comfort. In addition to miracles wrought, it is well known that you have used your inheritance for the common good. Many men would have succumbed to the temptation of riches, but Nicolaos of Myra has made of his an oblation."

Nicolaos looked upon his guest kindly. "The giver of every good and perfect gift has called upon us to mimic God's giving, by grace, through faith; and this is not of ourselves."[93]

"Well said," pronounced Alexander.

---

93 direct quotation attributed to Saint Nicholas

"There are many gathered here," Nicolaos said, "who have borne witness and received graces. I was humbled only this morning to meet Paul of Neocaesarea, who suffered untold agonies for our Lord."

"What happened to him?" asked Joseph.

"Because he would not deny his faith he was imprisoned, beaten, starved and mutilated. He is deprived of the use of both hands, for a red hot iron was applied to them. The nerves which give motion to the muscles were destroyed, leaving his hands scarred and useless. And still his heart beats strong for the Christ; his endurance is an inspiration. There are many such men, and many kinds of miracles."

He turned again to their guest. "Do not confuse what God may have accomplished through me with any attributes of mine. I am but a man, and I am shackled by my own flawed humanity."

How prophetic those words would prove to be.

LIX

The ecumenical[94] council convened on May 20 in the grand great marble hall of the imperial palace. Because only consecrated bishops were permitted access to the meeting chamber, Nicolaos appointed Alex as his assistant and keeper of notes, similar to the responsibilities granted Athenasius by the Bishop of Alexandria, so that Alex could be admitted to the chamber. Joseph was stationed with other deacons and presbyters on the balcony of an anteroom, where he might hear and see but not participate.

The emperor, Flavius Valerius Aurelius Constantine Augustus, wished to preside but would not arrive until mid-June. The priest Arius was to speak before the assembled council, but his appearance would be delayed until the arrival of Constantine, in whom he hoped to find a protector. Eusebius of Nicodemia, himself an open supporter of Arianism, gave a welcoming address. With Hosius of Corduba from Hispania, he would share in leading the discussion until the arrival of the emperor.

Preliminary talks were dominated by the Arian question, with debate becoming heated at times. Those on "the side of the Apostles" believed that Jesus was begotten and one with God the Father and the Holy Spirit. These believers included Alexander of Alexandria and his vocal, persuasive assistant Athenasius, Hosius of Corduba, historian Eusebius of Caesarea, the former hermit Jacob of Nisibis, Nicasius of Die from Gaul, Micarius of Jerusalem, several others, and of course Nicolaos of Myra.

In the Arian camp were Secundus of Ptolemais, Theonus of Marmarica, Paulinus of Tyre, and Theognus of Nicaea, among many others.

---

94 worldwide

The question of the identity and essence of Christ was of paramount importance, for only in orthodoxy, Nicolaos firmly believed, lay the salvation of souls. Nearly each day he contributed his arguments, countering those he considered heresy; and each evening he searched the face of Joseph for any indication that his arguments had held sway. The lad was young and earnest in his quest for truth, but guarded in his opinions. It seemed that he would not be moved to express them until his hero, the "independent thinker" of his day, appeared before the council to plead his views.

There were many other matters before the council, according to the agenda. They were to fix the date of the Christian Pasch, the commemoration of Christ's resurrection and the holiest of feast days to a Christian. Churches in the East had been linking it to the Jewish Passover and Feast of Unleavened Bread in the lunar month of Nisan, while those in the West were celebrating after the spring equinox, citing the increasingly unreliable calculation of Nisan in the Jewish calendar.

They were to discuss Melitius of Lycopolis and the so-called Melitian schism; decide whether men admitted to the clergy by Melitius—to include Arius, made a deacon by him—were validly ordained.

Many Church laws, or canons, were to be debated, including the minimum requirements for catechumens before baptism; vows of chastity; aspects of penance; the fate of those who had lapsed or repudiated the faith and later recanted; prohibition of usury and self-castration among clergy; and the proscription against kneeling, more appropriate to atoning prayer, on Sundays and at joyful Pasch.

All of these questions were being examined by the council but were not put to a vote. It seemed to Nicolaos that the assembly of bishops was accomplishing very little. It appeared that the majority did not wish to act decisively in the absence of the emperor who had called them together. He wondered whether they were forgetting that they were truly called by God, to shape a Church which did not include Constantine.

Nicolaos felt rising tension and the weight of indistinct foreboding as the days of the floundering council drew on. The delay distressed him, more so than it bothered Alexander or Joseph. He became restless, finding it difficult to sleep. With firm resolve he turned to fasting and prayer to restore his focus and to gain a measure of peace.

Surely the Holy Spirit would nurture and guide him and his brothers when the time came. Surely. And may the time come soon!

LX

The Emperor Constantine joined the proceedings of the great Council of Nicaea on the 14th of June at an hour when the sun was nearly at its zenith. As he entered the great hall to a fanfare of trumpets, strong light was behind him on the threshold, rendering him a tall and shadowy figure surrounded by radiance. As he proceeded ceremonially to the place of prominence on the dais it was as though he carried the light with him. He was arrayed in robes of shimmering purple and glittering gold, lavishly adorned with true gold and precious gems. Eusebius of Caesarea would record that he "proceeded through the midst of the assembly like some heavenly messenger of God, clothed in raiment which glittered, as it were, with rays of light."[95] With all the graciousness of an erudite statesman he respectfully called for the bishops to be seated before he himself regally took his seat between two armed Roman guards. His role would be that of overseer and presider, but he would not cast any vote. Hosius of Corduba, now President of the Council, introduced Eusebius of Nicomedia, who presented his second, more elaborate, welcoming address.

From his place near the dais Nicolaos studied the emperor with what he told himself was impartiality. Constantine had neither declared himself a Christian nor deigned to be baptized, so his motives were suspect, despite overtures of friendship to the Church to which his mother was devoted. Here was a man, Nicolaos reasoned, who knew how to govern disparate peoples and who recognized the advantage in supporting a growing religion whose very credo signaled peace and brotherhood. He also was a man who commanded

---

95 Eusebius of Caesarea, *Vita Constantini* (Life of Constantine), *Book 3, Chapter 10*

attention: pleasing in appearance, clean shaven and exhibiting a strong jawline, the embodiment of power and potency. From a distance his eyes could not be read, but Nicolaos observed that they raked the assembly with a remoteness that was chilling. He turned to look questioningly at Alex for his reaction and was rewarded with raised brows and a telling glance heavenward.

Constantine graciously acknowledged his welcome and exhorted the bishops to reach "unanimity and concord." He called upon them to follow Holy Scriptures, adding, "Let then all contentious disputation be discarded, and let us seek in the divinely-inspired Word the solution of the questions at issue."[96]

The first matter to be taken up before the emperor was the council's greatest question, that of Arianism. As its greatest proponent other than Arius himself, Eusebius of Nicomedia was invited to present the view that Jesus Christ was a created creature with free will, a finite being subservient to God the Father. Alexander of Alexandria summarized the opposing opinion, that Jesus was begotten, not made, one in essence with the Father, holding that the unity of the Godhead made the Son equal to the Father. The speeches were meant to be concise summations, but given each bishop's gift for oratory, the afternoon slowly wore on. Nicolaos was particularly sensitive to the passage of hours, for he was lightheaded from lack of sleep and food.

And then Arius himself was called to enter the great hall and address the emperor.

---

96 according to the historical writings of Theodoret (393-457), *Ecclesiastical History, Book 1, Chapter 6*

LXI

Arius of Libya and late of Alexandria entered the great hall with no fanfare, no formality of ceremony; but his arrival could not have been more momentous or stirring to those who had awaited him. They beheld a tall, spare individual who carried himself with an unmistakable air of superior self-possession. He was no longer young, although several years younger than Nicolaos. Yet there was a timelessness about his countenance, a quickness in his darting eyes, and a seductiveness in the Cupid's bow of a mouth which had heretofore persuaded so many. His garments were plain, as befit a renowned ascetic, but of fine cloth; and his protocol, as he made graceful obeisance to the emperor, was flawless. His manner revealed, Nicolaos decided, the finesse of a dancer well used to evading and refuting issues not to his liking.

Arius began to talk to the emperor and the assembly. He spoke in a melodious voice, loudly and slowly, for the benefit of those to whom Greek was foreign, with the reverence of one enamored of his own wit:

"God is inexpressible to all. We praise him as without beginning, in contrast to the Son, who has none of the distinct characteristics of God's own being; for he is not equal to, nor is he of the same being as God.

"The Father in his essence is a foreigner to the Son, who was made. The Son, not being eternal, came into existence by the Father's will. At God's will the Son has the greatness and qualities he has. His existence from when and from whom and from then—are all from God.

"God is inexpressible to the Son. The Son does not have understanding. It is impossible for him to fathom the Father, who is by himself, for the Son himself does not even know his own essence."[97]

It happened so quickly that even in retrospect Nicolaos was unaware of having chosen to act. He rose, strode to Arius, and struck him full across the face with the back of his hand.

A collective gasp went up throughout the great room. Constantine was immediately on his feet, exclaiming "Remove him!" The two Roman guards left the dais, grasped Nicolaos by the arms and fairly lifted his feet off the floor as they escorted him from the hall. Looking up, he saw Joseph agape, gripping the balcony rail, looking much like he had been stricken himself.

The great hall was in an uproar, abuzz with many competing conversations and several shouts of outrage, once the shock of the moment had passed. Eusebius of Nicodemia was ministering to Arius, who had taken the blow without losing his footing and was hurt only in his pride. The emperor called for a recess in the proceedings and retired quickly to a lower private antechamber, motioning the president of the council to follow.

"Who was that man?" he inquired of Hosius of Corduba.

"One of the bishops of Lycia to the south, Caesar. Nicolaos of Myra."

Constantine stopped abruptly, turning to Hosius. "Nicolaos? I know that name."

"Not surprising, Caesar."

---

97 Loosely compiled from Arius's *Thalia,* quoted in *De Synodis* by Athenasius, as translated by Hans-Georg Opiz (1905-1941) and others

A faint smile played upon the emperor's lips. "Yes. Yes, he is known to me. Sylvester's nuncio brought me the tale of this bishop saving three innocents from beheading, and his unmasking of the corrupt officials behind their supposed crime."

"I too recall hearing of the incident."

"He was seen to wrest the very sword from the executioner's hands."

Constantine accepted a goblet of wine from a servant, as did Hosius. "He is a man of passion, Hosius, and prone to impulse." Constantine drank and frowned; clearly the quality of Bithynian wine did not rival that of Rome.

Hosius hesitated. "When he is in the right, Caesar," he offered.

The emperor nodded. "That may be so. But we must have order. I will not have these proceedings disrupted again."

"Of course, Caesar."

"Keep him in irons—no, not in irons, but confined in isolation until the council is concluded."

"Yes, Caesar."

Constantine downed his wine. "Come, drink up. We have work before us."

LXII

"*Nico! Mea Nico!*"

The stale and fetid air within his prison cell was suddenly fragrant. Myrrh, if he were not mistaken, and . . . attar of roses.

Two figures were taking shape in growing light before him, one masculine, slender and tall, one smaller, feminine, and quite beautiful; and as their features became clearer he was nearly blinded by their radiance.

"My Lord! My Lady!"

Their voices were distinct and pure, resounding in his mind.

The Man said, "We come to thank you, dearest friend. Your conscience speaks to your generous heart, wherein I have always dwelt, and you act out of love. I bless you, Nico, and I tell you this: When you stand before the seat of God, loving Father of us all, you will obtain eternal life."

And the Woman said, "Yet in this world among men, and among the children of men, merely by living your great faith you shall achieve immortality, Nicolaos. Go in peace and grace."

✠

The vision was still fresh and confounding his senses when the iron door to his cell swung open. The light of day was without, and two men, familiars, had come to collect him. Alex and Joseph were staring at him strangely.

"Your face, Bishop!" Alex exclaimed in wonder, "It is burnished as with the sun, and your hair and beard are white."

Nicolaos found his voice, not used in many weeks. "I—I had a visitation. The Lord Jesus and his holy Mother spoke to me."

Young Joseph crossed himself and whispered, "Blest are the pure single-hearted, for they shall see God!"[98]

---

98 from the Beatitudes, Matthew 5:8 NAB, paraphrased

LXIII

They repaired to the rooms overlooking the lake, theirs at the expense of the empire for one more day. Alexander could hardly contain himself while Nicolaos washed and Joseph was sent for decent food.

"A triumph, your Honor! The council is at long last concluded; you are freed and so are we all. We have a new creed, and Arius is exiled!"

Washing the grime of confinement from his body, Nicolaos gazed at him with sincere dismay, wishing that disgrace could be so easily cleansed. "But sinner that I am, Alex, I have shamed you."

"Nay, it is not shame that I feel but pride; and if that be sin, my guilt is greater than yours! Many opinions were changed after you were dragged from the hall, Bishop! I think for the first time some of our brethren saw clearly the illusions spun by Arius, and they weighed the cost."

"And Joseph?"

Alex smiled. "Joseph found a new hero that day. If the arguments of his friend Athanasius did not persuade him, surely your boldness did. He has embraced the new creed with conviction."

"God be praised."

Refreshed with food and drink, clean and wrapped in a fresh tunic and scarlet robes, Nicolaos thanked his God, and God's mother, for untold blessings. He prayed silently while his friends respectfully waited, until a giddy smile came to his lips and he opened his eyes. "Read it again, please."

Alex stood by the window open to the view of water, to catch the waning light. He began:

"We believe in one God,

the Father almighty,

maker of all things visible and invisible;

And in one Lord, Jesus Christ,

the Son of God,

begotten from the Father, only-begotten,

that is, from the substance of the Father,

God from God, light from light,

true God from true God,

begotten, not made—"

"Amen," interjected Nicolaos.

"—of one substance with the Father,

through Whom all things came into being,

things in heaven and things on earth;

Who because of us men and because of our salvation came down,

and became incarnate and became man, and suffered,

and rose again on the third day, and ascended to the heavens,

and will come to judge the living and dead;

And in the Holy Spirit.

But for those who say, 'There was when He was not,

and, Before being born He was not,

and that He came into existence out of nothing,

or who assert that the Son of God is of a different hypostasis or substance,

or created, or is subject to alteration or change—

these the Catholic and apostolic Church anathematizes."[99]

"It is good," Nicolaos said. "It is very good."

Rejoicing, they drank a toast in wine to the new resolution, and one to the future of the Church, and another to Myra and another to their safe journey home. The shutters were drawn, and they made ready for the night's rest.

As the bishop reclined in comfort, and even as he was nearly lost to sleep, a smile remained on his face. "We must away on the morrow," he was heard to mumble. "I fear my dog misses me."

---

99 EarlyChurchTexts.com

LXIV

The years following the Council of Nicaea passed for Nicolaos at an accelerated rate, as we all perceive years tend to do when we are aging. He was grateful for overall good health but did not wish to test his stamina overmuch by traveling outside his see. He did have one more meeting with the Emperor Constantine, however. At the behest of all the people of Myra, he appealed to Constantine at Constantinople to decrease unfairly high taxes levied against them, and he was successful. The lower tax rate would remain in force for a century.

The scourge of Arianism was not eradicated with the exile of Arius and two of his unyielding supporters. It was generally understood that Eusebius of Nicomedia and two other bishops affixed their signatures to the creed adopted on June 19, 325 only in deference to the emperor, who wanted it. Constantine thereafter issued an edict: "If any writing composed by Arius should be found, it should be handed over to the flames, so that not only will the wickedness of his teaching be obliterated, but nothing will be left even to remind anyone of them. And I hereby make a public order, that if someone should be discovered to have hidden a writing composed by Arius, and not to have immediately brought it forward and destroyed it by fire, his penalty shall be death."[100] Even so, conflict between professed Arians and "Trinitarians" continued. As for Arius himself, he found refuge in Palestine and continued to preach as an outcast, omitting much—but not all—that the Church had found objectionable in his personal doctrine.

---

100 *"Edict by Emperor Constantine against the Arians,"* Fourth Century Christianity. Wisconsin Lutheran College.

Athenasius succeeded Bishop Alexander of Alexandria in 327, becoming a "boy bishop" in his own right. He remained adamant in his opposition to all that Arius stood for. Although the emperor never repudiated his edict, Constantine was committed to peace within the Church and ultimately allowed those exiled to return to their homes. Athenasius was condemned by the First Synod of Tyre in 335 for his rigidity. Arius was restored to communion by the Synod of Jerusalem in 336. Nicolaos attended neither synod.

Before he could be received at the cathedral in Constantinople and thus resume priestly duties, Arius attended a triumphal rally with his followers in Constantine Square. He was stricken with a hemorrhage of the bowels and excused himself from the festivities. He was later found dead in a lavatory, his entrails expelled. There were those who deemed the manner of his death to be divine retribution. Others suspected poison. Nicolaos asserted neither and prayed for the salvation of his soul.

It was also in the year 336 that the Emperor Constantine decreed that the birth of Christ would be observed on December 25. Most Christians believed this was a political expedient, to counter the pagan celebrations of the rebirth of Sol Invictus and the birth of Mithra on that date, and to appropriate the festive revels of Saturnalia.[101] Nicolaos did not mind nor question the emperor's motives. He was well versed in the writings of Africanus[102] which dated the conception of Jesus to March 25. Since the time of his childhood he had found that date easy to remember, because it was near his own birthdate. Given what he understood of the miracle of any human conception and birth, he felt such timing for celebration of his dearest Friend's birthday made good sense.

The following year Constantine was baptized on his deathbed by none other than Eusebius of Nicodemea, the old proponent of Arianism. It was said that the emperor waited until that eleventh hour in the belief that baptism

101 gift-giving feast of Saturn at winter solstice
102 Sextus Julius Africanus, 160-240 A.D. Greco-Roman traveler and historian

would release him from all sins committed during his reign. Nicolaos prayed for his soul.

LXV

Seasons of change and loss within his own circle were felt far more acutely than those on the world stage. The years were kind for the most part to those close to Nicolaos, those for whom his very breath was constant prayer. But life in its infinite possibility and death in its sweet inevitability marked time for him like the knelling of a sacred bell.

The first of many losses was the death of Arsenios, faithful friend and keeper of the purse, who slipped away moments after his "young master" anointed him. With him went the last living bond with his parents, particularly Epiphánios. Others shared ties with Patara and the yellow house of his childhood, but only Arsenios had served his father closely and known all the secrets of his business and his legacy.

Belsnickel was not a young dog when Emil brought him to Myra. But he was a youthful pup in spirit and steadfast in his devotion. When accompanying his reverend master on their strolls about the city became difficult, Clodio fashioned a cushioned barrow so that Peter might wheel Bels alongside the bishop, much to the delight of the children of Myra. By the time Belsnickel was gone, Nicolaos himself was slowing down, for his breath was often labored and the pain in his back and legs grew more severe. He was ready to spend more time in meditation.

No one knew for sure how old Black Peter was, not even Peter himself; for a former slave born into bondage there was little reckoning. Those who loved him knew only that he had the mind of a wizard, the instincts of an entertainer and the heart of a child. When he passed on to glory half the city came to the cathedral to honor his memory.

Not all transitions were melancholy. Alex grew in stature as a priest and was rewarded with his own church in nearby Limyra.[103] Nicolaos traveled there to bless the altar, accompanied by Clodio, Vivienne and several of their grandchildren, who took pleasure in the ferry ride and the masked clowns at the theater.

Young Joseph was indeed ordained a presbyter, and took Clodio's eldest daughter Irene to wife the same year. Wedding guests from Patera or from shared history in the underground came from many parts of Lycia. Their first child was a girl. At the baptism the bishop inwardly rejoiced and outwardly wept when Joseph proudly announced, "Her name is Mena."

"And so you are come," Clodio whispered. "My time must be near."

It was a moment Nicolaos had dreaded, and had called on the Lord to help him endure with grace. Candlelight flickered on the gay embroidery of the coverlet; there was a warm draft from an open window. Vivienne had taken care to keep the room immaculate and pleasant.

"It is a parting only for a short while, old friend."

"So you say. But God may say different. Sea turtles live long."

Nicolaos smiled through tears. "Ah, but this one has been blessed with long life already, Scorpion. I have gone far and seen amazing things."

"Did I not tell you?" His voice was weak but his eyes were bright, and his grip on his bishop's hand was strong.

"You did. Our Lord gave me a wise companion in you, Clodio."

"And you were my greatest gift."

---

103 Finike, Türkiye

As he prepared the oils and made ready to speak the sacramental words, it was with the bittersweet understanding that after this day what remained for him was interior life, a more solitary life in Jesus.

LXVI

Myra, December 6, 343 A.D.

Sleep was very near. It seemed to Nicolaos that he slept too much of late, but it could not be helped. His body lacked the stamina and resilience of youth; simply sitting still invited drowsiness. Sleep was peaceful; it was seductive. And there were dreams. Dreams that drew him to his bed, for in them he was young again, and all the dear souls departed from him were living.

As ever he did when on the verge of slumber, he examined his life in prayer. *Lord, I hope I have served you well today. I hope I have not injured or offended another soul; but if I have done so, sinner that I am, show me how to make amends and I will hasten to do your will. I wish to please you, for I have only gratitude, Lord, for your blessings and graces, and for the people you have placed in my path.*

They seemed to pass before him, parading through his consciousness, mirthful and adoring. He saw his parents and his uncle; himself as a youth and Clodio, sunning on rocks by the sea. He saw the fair sister of Clodio, yet a humble virgin; the three daughters of Demetrios, each a bride; the dear deaconess Mena. And children! Visions of children tumbled before his heavy eyelids, the little girls in the house of Abram, the boys in the barrel, the wards of the mission; the babe Joseph whom Mena loved so. The children of the streets, exultant to receive gifts, stories and coins. He could see himself in his fine red robe with Peter and Belsnickel, and the jubilant children. So many children.

Night had fallen, yet he heard birdsong. He felt himself rising, soaring, following the flight of a bird into morning light. It was the blackbird, always first to announce the dawning. He remembered now! It was his Nonna who called him Nico, her Nico. Dearest nurse, she was once everything to him. She was love.

And now here was perfect love, and music sweeter than birdsong, and light far greater than dawn.

"My Jesus!"

"*Mea Nico!*"

Saint Nicholas, pray for us!

EPILOGUE

In Western Christianity the Feast Day of Saint Nicholas of Myra is December 6, the day of his death. Eastern Rite Churches celebrate him on December 19; or on May 9, to observe the "translation," or relocation, of his relics. What is important is that he has been venerated as a holy saint throughout all of Christianity for well over 1,600 years. That is a fact.

There is recent archaeological evidence that Nicholas was entombed in a stone-cut church located at the highest point on the small island of Gemile, only twenty miles from his birthplace, Patara. The church was built in the fourth century around the time of his death, and his name is painted on part of the ruins. In antiquity this place was known as "Saint Nicholas Island," and today it is Gemiler Adasi, which means "Island of Boats." Saint Nicholas is one of the patron saints of seafarers and is the only major saint associated with that part of Türkiye.

In the seventh century the island was vulnerable to Arab attacks, so the saint's remains, contained in a sealed sarcophagus, were removed about 25 miles east to Myra, where he had served as bishop for most of his life. At Myra, once each year the relics exuded a clear, watery liquid that smelled like rose water. The liquid was called manna or myrrh, and was believed to possess miraculous powers.

In 1054 the Catholic Church in the West declared the Greek Church, at that time the official religion of the Byzantine Empire, in schism. By 1071 the Byzantine Empire had lost control of the area around Myra to invading Turks. Italian sailors from Bari in 1087 took advantage of the general confusion and the loss of Myra's Byzantine imperial protection. Over the objection of the Greek Orthodox monks there, they raided the cathedral and seized part—indeed most—of the remains of Saint Nicholas. They transported them to Italy, arriving in Bari on May 9, 1087. Whether unscrupulous thieves or heroic rescuers, the Italians safeguarded the partial remains, and two years later Pope Urban II personally placed them in the tomb beneath the altar of a new church in Bari, the Basilica di San Nicola.

At Bari the remains continued to produce "myrrh." A flask of manna is extracted from the tomb of Saint Nicholas every year on his feast day and is sold in vials in the basilica's shop. It is unclear whether the fragrant liquid originates from the remains within the tomb or from the marble tomb itself, as the tomb is below sea level. Many explanations have been proffered, including the transfer of seawater to the tomb by capillary action. Yet manna had been collected from the tomb of Saint Nicholas in Myra also for at least 250 years. That tomb was beneath his cathedral, which is under the present church in Demre, well inland. The earthly remains of a man who died over 16 centuries ago is the gift that keeps on giving. That too is a fact.

Saint Nicholas has always been immensely popular, and many other churches throughout the world claim to have relics of his, or small parts of his remains. In the 1950's while the crypt in Bari was undergoing restoration, the bones were removed from the sarcophagus for the first time since inter-ment, and with papal permission were examined by Luigi Martino, profes-sor of anatomy at the University of Bari, under the supervision of a special Pontifical Commission. Martino took thousands of measurements and made detailed scientific drawings, photographs and x-rays. These revealed that the man who died at over 70 years of age was of average height. In 2004 scientists at the University of Manchester, United Kingdom, reviewed Martino's data and further determined that the saint had been about five feet, six inches tall, was of slender to average build; that he had a broken nose which had healed, and that he suffered from severe chronic arthritis in his spine and pelvis. A facial reproduction was made, and in 2014 an updated reconstruction was made by the Face Lab at Liverpool's John Moores University. In 2017 two researchers from Oxford University radiocarbon dated a fragment of pelvis originally from a church in Lyons, France, at that time in the possession of a priest in Illinois. The bone was one of the oldest examined by the Oxford team and may well be from the remains of Saint Nicholas. That question may be answered by DNA testing at some future time.

Nearly all the legends about Saint Nicholas feature the pattern of three, the favorite number in folklore: Three maidens saved from prostitution, three boys in a brine or bran barrel, three innocents spared execution; in most versions of the famine story, there are even three ships of grain. No matter. Nicholas was called Wonderworker during his lifetime for a reason. Oral traditions don't materialize from nothing. There is always a kernel of truth behind them. The saint's saving of the condemned men and his negotiation of a tax reprieve for his city are well entrenched in historical tradition. And a great famine did take place in Lycia in 311-312.

Saint Nicholas is the patron saint of children, sailors, fishermen, merchants, the falsely accused, repentant thieves, brewers and barrel makers, pharmacists, archers, pawnbrokers, broadcasters, unmarried people; and students in many places throughout the world. Over time his legend has morphed into that of Santa Claus, Sinterklaas, Father Christmas; good old Saint Nick.

He was a holy man who was generous and good. That is surely a fact. Pray for us, Saint Nicholas of Myra!

GRAINS OF SALT AND LIBERTIES

This book is a work of fiction. There is little substantiated history of the life of Saint Nicholas of Myra. Some of the many traditional stories about him were told close to the time of his death, when he was known as The Wonderworker for all the miracles attributed to him; and still more were chronicled a couple centuries after he died, when there were already several churches bearing his name in tribute.

It is generally agreed that he was born in Patara in what is now Türkiye on March 15, 270 A.D., the only child of wealthy Greek Christian parents. He was said to be the nephew of a bishop, likely the Bishop of Patara. Some sources say his uncle was the bishop of Myra, the cleric he succeeded. Methodius—Hero-Martyr Methodius of the Orthodox Church, not St. Methodius of the Roman Catholic Church—was Bishop of Patara and lived until 312 A.D. Nicholas was 42 years old in 312, already Bishop of Myra himself. For the uncle who mentored and ordained him I chose Methodius, whose views on Christ and the Trinity mirror those of Nicholas in my telling of his story, and whose writings exist to the present day and may be quoted. The unusual manner of Nicholas's selection as bishop is a long held tradition.

The title? *Nicolaos* or *Nikolaos* is the Greek for Nicholas. I have used a Greek spelling of his name throughout. *Mea Nico* is Latin for "my Nico." Some authorities believe the saint's mother was Johanna and his father Epiphánios; others that his parents were Nonna and Theophánes. I have taken the liberty of choosing the former but included Nonna as a character important to Nicholas in infancy. It is also worthy of note here that the Greeks, unlike the Romans, did not use surnames.

Part of established Nicholas lore is that he was educated in the Scriptures from the age of five, had a natural piety, and encouraged his parents to pray and fast. When Nicholas was orphaned by a plague, he inherited riches which he shared generously. He was known to have visited the Holy Land before becoming bishop.

Nicholas is said to have destroyed several pagan temples in Myra. Recent archaeological excavations on the site of his cathedral in Demre (Myra) recently revealed the very mosaic tile floors on which the saint himself walked.

The existence of secret underground cities in Lycia is historical fact. One of the most extensive of these is currently being restored in hopes of becoming a major tourist attraction in Türkiye.

Nicholas is believed to have been imprisoned twice. First, during the persecution of Roman Imperator Diocletian, which began in 303 A.D. He was released sometime after Constantine came to power, probably about 310 A.D. Torture along with imprisonment was common. Examination of the saint's skull and his facial reconstruction in 2014 confirm a broken and subsequently asymmetrical nose.

Theodore the Lector's list of attendees at the Council of Nicaea in 325 A.D., one of the earliest lists made, records Nicholas as attendee number 151. In fact, he is mentioned in three early lists, but Theodore's is considered the most accurate. His name is conspicuously absent from the notes made by Athanasius of Alexandria, Bishop Alexander's assistant, and from later lists of participants. Legend has it that because he slapped "a certain Arian" across the face the Bishop of Myra was removed from the council, and that both Jesus and Mary appeared to him during his subsequent imprisonment.

The places in this book were well researched for authenticity to the time, as were the flora and fauna of ancient Türkiye and Palestine.

The characters in this book, other than Saint Nicholas and those identified by footnotes, are fictional. Because the saint's legacy is Santa Claus or

Father Christmas, and because in many cultures throughout the world his helpers or sidekicks have been Black Peter and Belsnickel, I wove character portrayals with those names into this book, just for fun. I think Saint Nick would have liked that.

A WORD OF THANKS

According to the Called and Gifted Program of the Catherine of Siena Institute, signs that you possess the charism of writing include "an unmistakable inner experience of peace, energy and joy while using the gift," and a "natural flow and ease" about the process. I can say without hesitation that for me, all that is true. Nothing makes me happier than creating a story that may help others feel closer to God. There was no writer's block whatsoever for me in imagining the world of Saint Genesius of Rome in *Genesius* or of Saint Nicholas of Myra in *Mea Nico*. Quite the contrary. I am in the habit of asking the Holy Spirit to guide me through the writing which brings me such joy, and somehow the words come.

I was a bit at sea after completing *Genesius* in 2021. I missed the daily routine of picturing myself inside the life of a saint, and writing about it. At Christmastime I was moved to research St. Nicholas and once again was intrigued. Here was a saint who was a contemporary of Genesius of Rome, but whose tradition did not consist of one simple conversion event and nothing else. It was a lifetime of extraordinary deeds and circumstances. Yet because of the popularity of his legacy, Santa Claus, nearly all the books about Saint Nicholas of Myra were for children. It seemed to me that the rest of us needed to know much more about the rest of him!

I am indebted to my advance reader Denise McCollum. It is always helpful to enlist fresh eyes to read a manuscript, and to gauge friendly yet impartial reactions. I am thankful for the encouragement of my brother and sister-in-law Tommy and Kathy Davis, my nephews and their wives, Dan and Katy Bowen Davis and Matt and Candice Davis; and to my grand-nephews

Brett and Beau for their inspiration in the portrayal of Nicolaos as a small child. I also wish to acknowledge the support of my friend Father Donald J. Rooney; my pastor Father John P. Mosimann; and many "fans" at St. Mary of the Immaculate Conception Catholic Church in Fredericksburg, Virginia, especially the faithful members of the Saint Mary Book Club. But most of all I am grateful to my collaborator, the Holy Spirit, who hears my pleas and gives me the words.

Donna Lee Davis became a writer at the age of eight, entertaining her mother and grandmother with hilarious stories (which were not meant to be funny) and reciting her original poetry at school assembly. She became a Roman Catholic in 1969 and began regaling heaven in earnest with gratitude and appeals for guidance in her vocation. After a long career in federal service at Quantico as chaplains' secretary and supervisory military court reporter, she accepted early retirement in 1999. Donna has devoted her time this century to church volunteer work and writing, lots of writing. She lives in Hartwood, Virginia.

https://donnaleedavis.com